AND THE

by NEILL CAMERON

FREDDY

AND THE

NEW KID

by NEILL CAMERON

David Fickling Books

With Special Thanks to Anthony Hinton and Katie Bennett

Freddy and the New Kid
is a
DAVID FICKLING BOOK

First published in Great Britain in 2021 by
David Fickling Books,
31 Beaumont Street,
Oxford, OX1 2NP

Text and illustrations © Neill Cameron, 2021

978-1-78845-164-2

1 3 5 7 9 10 8 6 4 2

The right of Neill Cameron to be identified as the author and illustrator
of this work has been asserted in accordance with the
Copyright, Designs and Patents Act 1988.

Papers used by David Fickling Books are from well-managed
forests and other responsible sources.

MIX
Paper from
responsible sources
FSC
www.fsc.org
FSC® C018072

DAVID FICKLING BOOKS Reg. No. 8340307

A CIP catalogue record for this book is
available from the British Library.

Printed and bound in Great Britain by Clays, Ltd, Elcograf SpA.

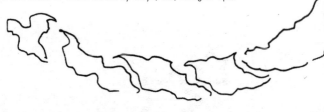

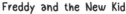

FOR LOGAN!

What up, humans! How is it going? You have probably already heard of me, because I am **PRETTY FAMOUS**, but just in case somehow you **HAVEN'T**, here are the main things you should know:

★ My name is ***FREDDY!***

★ I live in London with my mum and dad, and my big brother, Alex

★ I go to school

★ I am an ***AWESOME ROBOT***, with MANY AMAZING ROBOTIC ***SUPER-POWERS***!

What **KIND** of Amazing Robotic **SUPER-POWERS**, I hear you ask! Good question! Let me answer it in the form of an awesome **THEME SONG** I made up for myself:

I am made of **METAL**
Super-heavy **METAL, YEAH,**

I am **INDESTRUCTIBLE!**

And also I have **LASERS**
Awesome **LASERS**
LASERS AND **ELECTRIC BOLTS**

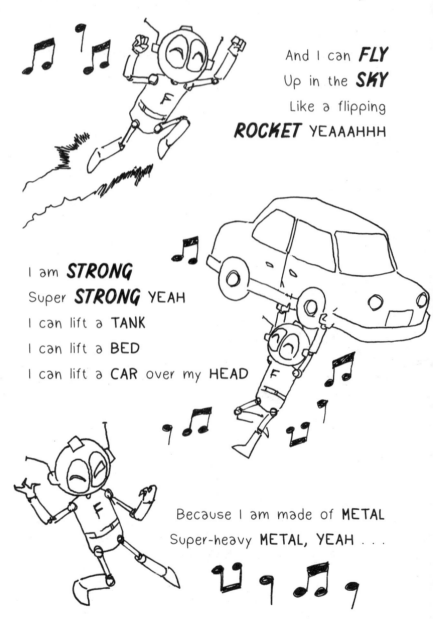

And I can **FLY**
Up in the **SKY**
Like a flipping
ROCKET YEAAAHHH

I am **STRONG**
Super **STRONG** YEAH
I can lift a **TANK**
I can lift a **BED**
I can lift a **CAR** over my **HEAD**

Because I am made of **METAL**
Super-heavy **METAL, YEAH** . . .

(Repeat until people yell at you to stop)

Anyway, even though I have all these amazing **SUPER-POWERS**, I am **NOT** supposed to use them at school. There have been certain **INCIDENTS**, like that one time Mr Javid's car got accidentally exploded with lasers and he got all upset, **EVEN THOUGH** I explained it was for the purposes of a SCIENTIFIC DEMONSTRATION.

I am the only robot **AT** my school! Well, except for my big brother, Alex. Me and Alex are, in fact, the only robots in the **WHOLE WORLD** who even have to **GO** to school.

There are lots of robots in the world — robots that build cars, robots that lift heavy stuff onto ships, robots that deliver your shopping or whatever —

but of all these robots, we are the only ones in the **WHOLE WORLD** who are **SENTIENT.**

My mum is always trying to explain what this means to me. She says:

"Most robots just obey their programming, carrying out specific instructions. But you and Alex . . . you have **MINDS.** You're **CONSCIOUS. SELF-AWARE.** Which means you get to choose your own instructions. You're **FREE.**"

. . . except, as I pointed out, not **THAT** free, because I have to go to **SCHOOL.**

School is not **COMPLETELY 100%** terrible. Sometimes we get pizza for lunch! But **ALSO,** it is where my **FRIENDS** are.

Because of being a robot and everything, I am kind of **FAMOUS** at school, and my best friends are all members of my cool **TEAM ROBOT** gang.

So, yeah. Even though they don't have **LASERS** or ***ROCKET BOOSTERS***, humans can actually be quite cool.

Or so I thought. Until . . .

The day that everything changed.

CHAPTER

THE NEW KID...

. . . is called **AOIFE**, and she just started at our school this term, and she is **VERY ANNOYING**. Here are my . . .

TOP 5 ANNOYING THINGS ABOUT AOIFE

1 Her name. Pronounced 'eef-er'. It is Irish, apparently. My language circuits must not be set for Irish, because the whole first week she was at our school it kept giving me **MALFUNCTIONS**

2 Thinks she is **BETTER** than everyone — at **SPORT**, at **MATHS**, at all kinds of stuff

3 **VERY** annoyingly, **SHE IS IN FACT BETTER THAN EVERYONE AT ALL THOSE THINGS**

4 Never went to school with a robot before, so is always coming out with **NONSENSE**. For example . . .

5 The big one: Thinks **HUMANS** are better than **ROBOTS!?!?**

". . . Humans **are** better than robots," said Aoife. "I mean, that's just a Fact."

We were all out in the playground at break, and we were having a Disagreement.

"That's crazy!" I shouted. "Robots are obviously better than humans! I LITERALLY HAVE *LASERS!*"

"Maybe we could just agree," said Riyad nervously, "that robots are awesome and that humans are . . . also awesome?"

"NO!" me and Aoife both shouted together, and Riyad went "eeep" and jumped to hide behind a bin.

"Maybe you guys should **SETTLE** it," said Fernando. "Like, with a **CONTEST**."

"Great idea!" I said. "How about a **BLOWING THINGS UP WITH _LASERS_** contest? Or a **FLYING USING YOUR _AMAZING ROCKET BOOSTERS_** contest?"

And Aoife looked really annoyed, and that was very enjoyable.

"Well, that wouldn't really be fair, would it?" said Anisha, thoughtfully. "I mean, to be fair it would have to be stuff you can both do . . ."

Riyad poked his head out from behind the bin and joined in, "And to make it really fair you'd have to design a range of tests, across different aspects – mental, physical, and . . ."

"Like a **GAME SHOW!**" said Fernando. "Three challenges, three rounds!

And we'll make them up ourselves, and if Freddy wins, the robots are **OFFICIALLY THE BEST!**"

"Fine with me," I said, "because I **WILL** win!"

"Fine with **ME**," said Aoife, "because you **WON'T!**"

"But who would set the challenges?" Riyad asked. "It would have to be someone impartial, who could act as a judge . . ."

And everyone kind of turned and looked at Anisha expectantly, because everyone knows she can be trusted with this kind of thing.

"As long as I get a cool title," said Anisha.

So Anisha was appointed . . .

UGH.
FINE.

"And we'd have to have some **RULES**," said Anisha, looking thoughtful. "To make sure it's a fair contest . . ."

"Oh, not this," I muttered.

And we all looked over at the side of the school hall, where they have this big sign stuck up on the wall . . .

USE OF SUPERHUMAN
ROBOTIC ABILITIES IS

STRICTLY FORBIDDEN

ON SCHOOL GROUNDS

YES THIS MEANS **YOU**, FREDDY!

. . . because of certain, uh, incidents.

". . . No, I don't care about that," said Anisha.

"So I get to use my **LASERS** and stuff?" I asked, excited.

"What?" cried Aoife. "That's not fair!"

"But that's the point, isn't it?" said Anisha. "If we're seeing who's better, humans or robots . . . then Freddy should be allowed to do his . . . robot stuff. We'll just need to make sure the teachers don't see."

"Ha!" I said, and Aoife looked really annoyed, which was **GREAT**.

"There's just **ONE** rule," said Anisha. "You can use your powers, Freddy. But you can't use them against Aoife."

"What did you **THINK** I was going to do, **SABOTAGE** her with **LASERS** or something?" I said.

"Basically, yes," said Anisha. "Is everyone happy with that?"

"SUPER happy," said Aoife, scowling at me.

"ULTRA super happy," I said, scowling RIGHT BACK . . .

It was the next day at lunch, and everyone was getting impatient to find out what the first **HUMANS VS ROBOTS** challenge would be.

Okay, when I say "everyone" I mostly mean . . . me.

"What's it going to be?" I asked Anisha. "Huh? What's it going to be? Huh? Huh? **WHAT'S IT GOING TO BEEEE?**"

"Jeez, Freddy!" shouted Anisha. "I **TOLD** you, I haven't decided yet. Honestly, it is hard enough to think of these things without you **BUGGING** me all the time."

"Whatever it is," said Fernando, "I bet Freddy **WINS**."

And we did our special . . .

"Bet he doesn't," said Henrik, who was lurking around nearby, probably waiting for a chance to Break Something Or Hit Somebody.

"What are you talking about?" said Fernando. "Freddy is an **AWESOME ROBOT!**"

"Yeah," said Henrik, "but you know what that Aoife girl's like, she's captain of the football team, she's a total brainiac . . . I reckon she'll smash it."

"Bet she doesn't!" said Fernando.

"Yeah? What do you bet?" said Henrik.

Fernando reached into his lunchbox and pulled out a **CHOX** bar. "This!" he said. "One Chox says Freddy wins."

And Henrik's eyes lit up, because if there is one thing Henrik loves even more than Breaking Things And Hitting People, it is chocolate bars.

"You're on!" he said, grinning.

"You're going to bet **AGAINST** me?" I asked Henrik, **OUTRAGED**.

"Well, yeah," said Henrik. "Because you're going to **LOSE**."

"**THAT IS IT!**" I shouted. "**TREACHERY!** You are not allowed in **Team Robot** any more!!"

Henrik just shrugged. "Fine," he said. "Guess I'll go be on Team Human. And **WIN**."

And he just grinned and **WALKED OFF**, the absolute **TRAITOR**.

As it turned out, we didn't have to wait long to find

out what the challenge was. That afternoon, we all got to go to the local pool for our **SWIMMING LESSON**. And while we were all lined up waiting to go in the pool, Anisha suddenly said, "Okay, listen up. It is time for . . ."

THE FIRST CHALLENGE!

"What, here?" I said. "At the **POOL?**"

"Yes," said Anisha. "It is a **PHYSICAL** challenge. **A RACE!** You both have to swim **FOUR LENGTHS** of the big pool, and whoever comes first is the winner."

"Fine with **ME**," said Aoife, grinning. And **OF COURSE** she was grinning, because **OF COURSE** she is super great at swimming and has won contests and has actual **TROPHIES** and stuff.

"That's not fair!" I said. "She is really good at swimming! And I . . ."

". . . am a **_HIGHLY SUPERIOR ROBOT_**, right?" said Aoife. "What's the matter, are you scared you might lose?"

And I couldn't really say anything because then it would look like I **WAS** scared, and basically I had fallen right into her **CLEVER TRAP**.

"As **IF!**" I said. "Fine! I don't care! Let's **DO** it."

So **FIRST** we had to distract the teachers. There was one lifeguard watching the lesson, and Mr Latif, our P.E. teacher from school.

So we huddled together and came up with a quick **PLAN**, which was:

. . . Fernando got rid of the lifeguard by telling him he had to **COME QUICK**

because someone was having **EXPLOSIVE DIARRHOEA** in the splash pool, and meanwhile:

. . . Henrik told Mr Latif that Fernando had gone **MISSING** and must have got lost and wandered off into town.

"Oh, for . . . **NOT AGAIN!**" shouted Mr Latif, running out. "Everyone go and wait in the changing rooms until I get back. **NO** getting in the pool, okay?"

So we waited until he'd gone . . . and then got in the pool, obviously. Aoife and me had a lane each, and everyone else gathered round along the sides of the lanes to watch.

"Come on, Aoife!" shouted Henrik. "Team Human! Smash him!"

"Hey!" I said. "I am **RIGHT HERE.**"

"What?" said Henrik. "I've got a **CHOX** riding on this."

Anisha stood in the middle. "Okay!" she said, "Four lengths, whatever stroke you like. Fastest time wins! Ready . . . steady . . . **GO!**"

We both **PUSHED OFF** from the wall and started swimming! And **OF COURSE** Aoife got off to a great start. She was doing a proper front crawl, kicking with her legs, hardly making any splash at all . . .

. . . just generally going really **FAST** and making it look **EASY**.

I, meanwhile, was . . .

I **HATE** swimming, it is **STUPID** and **HARD**. For one thing, I am made of **METAL**, and so I have to work harder than everyone else just so **I DON'T SINK**. The whole thing is basically **TOTALLY UNFAIR**. And you have to move your arms and legs all together at the right times and in the right way and **LOOK**, it is just **HARD**, OK?

It is the kind of thing my mum is always going on about, about how I need to "practise" and "hone my abilities" or whatever. But I **HATE** practising, it is **BORING**. And the way I see it, why do I need to "hone my abilities"? So what if I am not super-great at swimming, or whatever, I can **LITERALLY PUNCH A HOLE IN A TANK**.

Anyway, I was trying to do a front crawl like Aoife, but it was coming out more like a doggy paddle. And to be honest, more like a doggy paddle if the dog had like **RABIES** or something. And had **GONE MAD**. And also **COULDN'T SWIM**.

I was definitely doing a lot of **SPLASHING**, but I didn't seem to actually be moving very fast. Or at all.

"Try and kick more with your legs!" I heard Riyad shout, unhelpfully.

"DON'T TELL ME WHAT TO DO!" I shouted back, and then sank under the water.

When I bobbed up again I could see that I had **BARELY MOVED**, and a bunch of the kids in the lanes were all **LAUGHING**.

Which made me really angry. And then I saw that Aoife was nearly at the end of the pool. She'd done a whole length already, while I'd barely started! And that made me even **ANGRIER**. She was going to win!

Unless . . . I did something about it.

CHAPTER 3

It looked like Aoife was going to **WIN** the first challenge! Just because, okay, **FINE** . . . she was **BETTER THAN ME AT SWIMMING.**

But I had one thing going for me that she didn't. And that thing was . . .

ROCKET BOOSTERS!

If I fired them off, I could shoot through the water at 200 miles an hour like a flipping **TORPEDO!**

And so that . . .

. . . **WAS EXACTLY WHAT I DID.**

I set my *ROCKET BOOSTERS* to . . .

... and I **SHOT** straight up the lane!

FWOOSH!!!

I went all the way to the other end in like two seconds flat! I **JUST** managed to slow down in time so that I didn't **SMASH** into the side of the pool. I turned round quickly, and fired off my **ROCKET BOOSTERS** again to come back.

And the best part was, Aoife had only just started her second lap, so I **WHIZZED** right past her so fast that she got splashed in the **FACE** by a massive **WAVE**.

It was
PRETTY
AWESOME.

I was making **LOTS** of waves now. All the kids who were watching were getting tossed up and down in the churning water like they were in a **WASHING MACHINE**. There was lots of clapping and cheering and also **SCREAMING**. But, you know, the happy kind of screaming.

I got back to the start and turned again and started **LENGTH THREE!**

I caught a glimpse of Aoife's face, looking really **ANNOYED**. So obviously, that was pretty great. To annoy her even **MORE**, I decided to really show off on my last length and **WIN IN STYLE**. I turned onto my back and folded my hands behind my head, so it looked like I couldn't even be bothered to stay **AWAKE**.

And I fired off my
ROCKET BOOSTERS
for the final length.

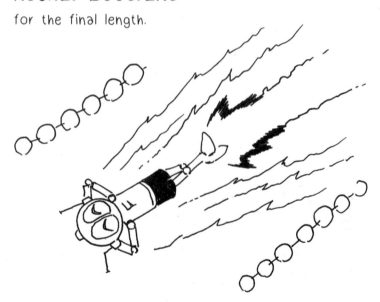

It is always good to defeat your enemies, but it is even **BETTER** to do so while **ANNOYING THEM MASSIVELY**.

Anyway, I must have been halfway along, with just half a length between me and **GLORIOUS VICTORY,** when suddenly I noticed that I could hear screaming. And this time it didn't sound like the happy kind, but the **ACTUALLY TERRIFIED** kind? I opened my eyes and saw . . .

RIYAD!

I must have drifted out of my lane and into the lane where all the spectators were bobbing around in the waves — and now I was heading straight for him! At like two hundred miles an hour!

Riyad is pretty small and also, y'know, a **HUMAN.** I didn't know exactly what would happen if he got hit by an ***INDESTRUCTIBLE ROBOTIC TORPEDO*** GOING AT TWO HUNDRED MILES AN HOUR . . . but I assumed it would be BAD. I barely had time to think . . .

I **QUICKLY** swerved my legs to change direction . . .

. . . but I was going so **FAST** that I kind of **FLIPPED**

out of the water like a jumping fish . . .

FLEW

through the air, out of control . . .

. . . and

CRASHED

down into the bin where they keep all the floats!

I was just getting my head together and trying to figure out which way was **UP** when I heard the sound of clapping and cheering and Anisha's voice shouting . . .

AOIFE WINS!

"What?" I shouted. "No way! I was way ahead of her! I **LAPPED** her!"

Aoife looking all smug and superior. Anisha looked at me. "Yeah, but Freddy," she said, "you didn't touch the side, so you didn't technically finish. Aoife did."

"That is **SO UNFAIR!**" I shouted.

Just then, Fernando walked back in from distracting the lifeguard. He looked at the scene, and at me still half-buried under a pile of floats, and asked "What happened?"

"You owe me a **CHOX**, that's what happened," grinned Henrik. "It's . . ."

TEAM HUMAN | TEAM ROBOT

1 | 0

And there was a lot of cheering.

And Aoife just **SMIRKED** at me.

And now I was **REALLY** annoyed.

CHAPTER 4

In assembly the next day, Mr Javid, the Deputy Head, said he had a **BIG ANNOUNCEMENT**. He was standing up at the front of the gym like normal, but next to him there was this big **SHEET** that was draped over . . . **SOMETHING**, but we couldn't see what.

Mr Javid is always telling me off and giving me detentions and calling my mum into school to have **Little Talks**, so I worried for a second that he'd found out about the swimming contest and maybe under the sheet he had a **TANK**, or possibly the **POLICE**.

"Due to certain . . . recent events, and unplanned expenses in the school budget . . ." he said, and he paused and **GAVE A LOOK**, right at where I was sitting.

"He means his **CAR** exploding," Fernando whispered to me.

"Sssshh!" I whispered. "We swore never to talk about that!"

". . . it has become necessary to find ways to make the school even more . . . financially competitive . . ."

"He means they need to save money," whispered Fernando.

". . . so as part of this bold new initiative to reduce our salary expenditure . . ."

"He means sacking teachers," whispered Fernando.

". . . we will be introducing . . ." said Mr Javid, and he pulled the sheet away . . .

. . . and underneath there were all these **ROBOTS**!

They looked like pretty basic robots, not super-awesome ones like me. They had like **SCREENS** for heads, showing like a cartoon emoji of a smiley face, and the one in the middle said **"BEEP! HEY GUYS, LET'S LEARN!"**

Immediately the whole gym exploded into noise. A lot of the kids were pretty excited by the idea of **Robot Teachers**, and a lot were laughing. But I looked around and not everyone was laughing. And some of the teachers were definitely not laughing. In fact Miss Obasi, our class teacher, looked really cross.

"These cutting-edge Educational Support Robots will be helping to take some of your classes. To begin with, only in . . . ahem, non-core subjects . . . Arts, P.E. and such . . ."

Anisha's big brother Nikesh, who is captain of the cricket team, put his hand up. "Sir, these are going to be our P.E. teachers? What about Mr Latif?"

Mr Latif is our P.E. teacher and he is pretty nice and

funny and sometimes if he trips or gets hit with a ball, or something, he will say **AMUSING SWEARWORDS**.

"Mr Latif . . . will not be returning. Replacing human teachers with these units will allow us to make significant savings, which will allow us to make improvements across the school . . ."

. . . and he went on and it was all **BLAH BLAH EXCELLENCE BLAH BLAH ACADEMIC ACHIEVEMENT** and whatever, but it was hard to hear him over the general noise. The teachers were all talking amongst themselves and seemed really cross, and Miss Obasi got up and just walked straight out while he was still talking.

Mr Javid tried to get everyone to quiet down but it was too late, everyone was a bit overexcited about the new **Robo-Teachers**, and Mr Latif being fired, and everything. And even though the whole thing was nothing to do with me, I couldn't help but notice a lot of people were looking at me.

And . . . not in a good way.

At break time the next day, everyone was still talking about the **Teacher-Bots**. "It might be cool," said Riyad. "I heard they're using them in lots of places now, and exam scores have gone up by 12% on adjusted average . . ."

"Ugh, nerd," said Henrik. Anisha glowered at him.

But not everyone was convinced. Aoife was going on about how rubbish they looked, and that got us arguing again about Who Is Better, Humans or Robots? And so of course **THEN** she started boasting about how she was winning the challenge 1-0, and how this just **PROVED** that she was right.

"I've had **ENOUGH** of this," I shouted. "Anisha, what

50

is the next challenge? I am going to **DESTROY** her at it."

A lot of people who were standing around near us in the playground heard this, and it was like all their ears perked up and they wandered over to listen. Word had got out about the Swimming Pool Incident, and Henrik had started taking bets on who was going to win the **NEXT** challenge, so people were eager to find out what it was going to be.

Anisha could see she had a bit of a crowd forming, so she put on her most dramatic voice and said:

"The next challenge . . . will be a . . ."

". . . Yeah, but **WHAT**, exactly?" I asked.

Anisha looked a bit shifty. "I . . . haven't decided yet."

"Well, hurry up!" I said, because frankly I was getting a bit impatient to **DEFEAT AOIFE** and **PROVE ROBOTS ARE THE BEST** and **NOT LISTEN TO HER NONSENSE ANY MORE**.

"I am doing my best!" said Anisha, looking annoyed. "It is actually quite hard coming up with ideas, you know."

"Pfff, it doesn't look hard to me," I said. "I bet I'd be **GREAT** at it."

"Oh yeah?" said Anisha. "Go on then!"

And everyone looked at me. And I couldn't think of **ANYTHING**.

"That's not my job, is it?" I protested. "You're Ultimate Challenge Adjudicator, that's **YOUR** job. Although it seems to me you're not very **GOOD** at it."

"Alright, that's **IT!**" shouted Anisha, looking really annoyed now. "You want an idea? Here's an idea. You know how we've got a Maths test in class tomorrow?"

TWITCH!

"Um, yes?" I said, worrying that I really might have pushed her too far.

"That's it," she said. "That's the challenge. Whoever gets the highest score on their Maths test wins."

"**AND,**" she added quickly, because she could see me starting to gesture to the crowd, "that is my **FINAL DECISION** and there will be **NO DEBATE.**"

And then Anisha stomped off, and Aoife followed after her, and I was left standing there feeling like I might have played that a bit wrong.

Henrik was running round taking bets all over and writing everything down in a little book. He was getting really into it. I think maybe he has a **GAMBLING PROBLEM**, or possibly a **CHOCOLATE BAR PROBLEM**, or possibly **BOTH**.

"How come you're not betting?" I asked Fernando, nudging him.

And he looked a bit embarrassed, and just said "Well, y'know, Freddy . . . it's Maths."

"Hey!" I shouted.

"Oh, fine," said Fernando, opening up his lunchbox and pulling out a whole **FAMILY PACK** of Chox. **"EIGHT CHOX ON FREDDY TO WIN."**

And everyone went, "Ooooooh". And Henrik's eyes lit up, and he wrote it down in his little book.

"Where did you get a whole family pack from?" I whispered to Fernando.

"My mums were both working this morning, so they told me to pack my own lunch," said Fernando. "So . . ." And he shrugged.

So now there was a lot riding on this. Like, honour and reputation and stuff, but also a **LOT** of chocolate bars. I had to win. I had to. The only problem was, if there is one thing I am even worse at than . . .

. . . well, than **BASICALLY ANYTHING**

. . . it is Maths.

The next day in class, Miss Obasi was handing out the Maths tests. She gave me mine and I had a quick look to check if somehow it was just a whole page of like "what is 2+2" over and over, which was basically my only hope.

But **NO**, of **COURSE** it was all **LONG DIVISION** and **DECIMAL PLACES** and, ugh, **FRACTIONS**.

TOP 5

DAYDREAMS I HAVE HAD WHEN I WAS SUPPOSED TO BE LEARNING MATHS

1 Me and my friends getting turned into SUPERHEROES and having to fight EVIL CYBORG MR JAVID

2 Me and my friends getting transported into SPACE and all getting GIANT ROBOT SUITS like in the TV show *Star Norse* and BLOWING THINGS UP with them

3 Me getting somehow turned into a **GIANT MONSTER** and stepping on the whole school like a **GODZILLA**

4 Me getting sucked into a parallel universe where instead of **HUMANS** there are **SENTIENT DOUGHNUTS**

5 Aoife getting EATEN BY DINOSAURS

Aoife is **OF COURSE** totally brilliant at Maths, and **OF COURSE** always comes top in class tests, and **OF COURSE** got a special prize in assembly one time for Outstanding Excellence In The Field of Maths.

I knew it was all over. Aoife would win, and then it would be **HUMANS 2, ROBOTS 0**, and I would have lost the whole thing! And Aoife turned round in her chair and **SMIRKED** at me, and started writing on her test. **Of COURSE** she was going to win, because **OF COURSE** she is so Naturally Brilliant at Maths. I didn't have a **HOPE**. I couldn't get through this one just by going **MAXIMUM POWER**.

And then I thought . . . maybe I could? If it was . . .

MAXIMUM
(COMPUTING)
- IIIIIIIIII +
POWER!

See, the thing is, and I may have mentioned this already, but I am an **AWESOME ROBOT**. Which means my brain is **LITERALLY** a computer. So even though I find Maths really hard and confusing and **JUST INSANELY BORING**, I have all these built-in Programs and Subroutines that, if I turn them on, can work out all the answers **FOR** me. It is basically like someone using a calculator app on their phone, which we are Strictly Not Allowed To Do in tests. But in my case, it's like the phone is **INSIDE MY HEAD**, so how could anyone really stop me?

I have asked my mum about this, **MANY TIMES:**

Why do I even have to bother learning maths in the first place? Why can't I just let the app in my head do it **FOR** me?

"You're supposed to be learning things yourself, not just relying on tricks. I mean, goodness, you've got an auto-translation app you could use and never have to take another French lesson, if it comes to that . . ."

. . . and I said, "Wait, **WHAT**, how do I use **THAT** and **WHY AM I SITTING THROUGH FRENCH LESSONS**, this is **INSANE!**"

And she said: "Freddy . . . the whole point of going to school is to learn. And not just the stuff in lessons, but so much more. How to learn, how to grow, how to . . . be a person, a part of the world . . ."

But to be honest by then I'd kind of stopped listening because I'd discovered the auto-translation app and was busy looking up rude words in French.

FREDDY TEACHES FRENCH!

★ "Caca" . . . means . . . POO!

★ "Pipi" . . . means . . . WEE!

★ "Pet Monstre" . . . means . . . FART MONSTER!

Anyway, the point is, I'm really not supposed to use my calculator app in school. And definitely not in tests. I'm supposed to do everything the "human" way.

But what is the point in that? I'm just sitting there staring at a whole page of symbols and numbers that don't make **ANY** sense, and how is that helping **ANYONE?** I looked at Aoife, scribbling away furiously, and I thought . . .

. . . it wouldn't be **CHEATING**. Like, Aoife is Naturally Brilliant at doing Maths, right? It is not cheating for her to use her natural abilities. It would just be . . . me using my natural abilities.

Anyway, even if it was against the school rules, who cared about that. It wasn't against the us rules, the rules for the contest. Anisha literally said I **WAS** allowed to use my powers. So it was fine.

And I thought about it again to check that that made sense, and it totally did.
And so . . .

BOOP!

. . . I turned on my calculator.

CHAPTER 7

"He must have **CHEATED!**" shouted Aoife.

It was break time, a couple of days later, and we had just got the results of our Maths tests back.

QUESTION: What has two thumbs and got the Highest Score In The Whole Class?

ANSWER:

I was careful to deliberately answer a couple of questions wrong, because I figured if I got them **ALL** right it might look **SUSPICIOUS**. Of course Aoife was **FURIOUS**, which was **VERY ENTERTAINING**.

"You don't like it when someone's better than **YOU** at something for once, do you?" I asked, feeling **VERY PLEASED** with myself.

"Because you're **NOT!** Because you must have **CHEATED!**" said Aoife.

"That is **QUITE OFFENSIVE** actually," I said. A bit of a crowd had gathered around us on the playground, eager to find out the result of the Second Challenge.

"If you do well it's cause you're really clever, but if someone else does well it must because they **CHEATED?**"

And there was a general **MURMUR** of agreement from the crowd that this was an **UNFAIR** and **TERRIBLE** attitude on Aoife's part, and she ought to be **PRETTY ASHAMED** of herself.

"Because you **DID**," she snarled, not buying it at **ALL.**

"How am I supposed to have cheated? We were all sitting in there together — could I have copied the answers without anyone seeing?"

And there was a general murmur of "no"s.

"Could I have somehow snuck a **CALCULATOR** in without anyone seeing?"

And there was another murmur of "no"s.

"There you are then. How am I supposed to have cheated?"

And Aoife looked just **HILARIOUSLY CROSS**, but she didn't have an answer to that.

And then a voice said "Well . . ." and we all looked round to see who it was. And, surprisingly, it was **RIYAD**.

". . . you could always have used the calculator app in your head," said Riyad.

"The what?" asked Aoife.

"Freddy has a bunch of onboard optional Augmented-Reality applications," carried on Riyad happily, ". . . maps, translation software and of course, high-level computing functions. Basically it's like having a calculator in his head."

"I knew it!" shouted Aoife. "So he **DID** cheat!"

"Riyad!" I shouted. "That was **SECRET TEAM ROBOT INFORMATION!**"

"But . . . but . . ." said Riyad, looking confused.

Riyad knows more than anyone about how my robotic systems work. He is very interested in **SCIENCE** so he is always asking me questions, and I am always happy to let him because it means I get to talk about **MYSELF**. I think he just thought it was an Interesting Scientific Fact. It hadn't occurred to him that **I might not want everyone to know about this**.

"I . . . I just thought it was interesting . . . " said Riyad.

"That's it!" I shouted at Riyad.

"You are **OUT** of Team Robot forever!"

"But . . . but . . ." said Riyad.

". . . So it doesn't count!" said Aoife. "Because Freddy cheated."

"It's not cheating though!" I shouted. "It's just me using what's in my head! Same as her! That's the whole point!"

And everyone looked at Anisha. And she looked thoughtful for a minute, and then said, "He's right."

"What?!" yelled Aoife, and Henrik, and all the people who'd bet chocolate bars on her.

"He was just using what's in his head," continued Anisha. "The whole point of the contest is to show who's better, humans or robots. Right? And if it turns out Freddy's literally got a calculator in his head, then I guess this is one where robots just are better. We said he was allowed to use his powers, we just . . . didn't know that was one of them. It's a bit sneaky, but it's not against the rules."

"The score is . . ."

"Judge's decision is final!" said Anisha.

And Aoife stomped off angrily, and Henrik started happily collecting all the chocolate bars from everyone who had bet against me. And Fernando was the **ONLY ONE** who'd bet on me, and he collected his **MASSIVE PILE** of Chox bars, and he shared them with me and they **TASTED LIKE VICTORY**.

I was just enjoying this **AMAZING MOMENT** when Miss Obasi walked over and said, "Freddy, can you come with me? We need to have a little talk."

Which didn't seem good.

And then she led me off on my own, and I realised we were heading to Mr Javid's office.

Which didn't seem good, either.

And then she opened the door, and sitting in there, looking **VERY UNHAPPY**, were Mr Javid and . . . my mum.

Which didn't seem good at all.

CHAPTER 8

"Aaah!" I shouted. "What's going on? Is this a
TRAP?!"

Mum rolled her eyes.

"It's not a trap, Freddy," said Miss Obasi. "I just
thought it would be good for us all to have a little
talk . . . about the Maths test."

Miss Obasi was being very **NICE** and **KIND** about it all, but I could tell something was up. And then she pulled out some **CHARTS**, and I knew I was in trouble.

"You see, Freddy," she said, "normally in Maths your scores are round about here . . ."

". . . but on the last test they were suddenly up **HERE** . . ."

. . . and OK, fine, when you look at it like that it maybe sticks out a bit.

They all took turns to tell me how I'm really not supposed to use my apps in school, and how it's not fair to everyone else, and how disappointed in me they were, and . . .

If there is one thing I am not a super big fan of, it is having to sit and listen to people **TELL ME HOW TERRIBLE I AM**. So I stopped.

Another little trick I can do, see, is control the volume levels on my hearing. So I can turn it all the way up and have **SUPER MEGA ROBO HEARING**, and hear what people are saying all the way at the other end of the football pitch. Or I can turn it all the way down, and basically put the world on Mute.

Which is what I did.

I could see them all making their annoyed faces and jabbering away all **BLAH BLAH BLAH FREDDY THIS IS TERRIBLE**, but at least I didn't have to actually listen to it. I just made a Sad Face — because obviously that was all they really wanted to see — and let them go nuts.

While they were all banging on about **WHATEVER**, I just had a nice daydream about what it would be like if the school got taken over by zombies and I had to shoot them all with *LASERS*.

Eventually we got to go, and all the way home on the tube Mum was giving me Cross Looks, but I just kept the world on mute and happily murdered zombies inside my head.

When we got home Mum stomped off to her lab, and I went up to my room, and climbed under my duvet to make an Ultimate Fortress of Isolation where **NO ONE WAS ALLOWED IN** and I could be **LEFT ALONE**.

But then the lights came on, and someone had come in,

and it

was Dad.

He lifted up the duvet, and he made a "turn the dial up" gesture with his hand. Somehow Dad always knows when I have Muted everyone. But I still didn't feel like listening to anyone, so I didn't.

He just gave me a Dad Look, and I turned the volume back up.

". . . Oh, hello Freddy," he said. "Thank you for joining us, finally. I just want to talk to you for a minute."

"If it is about how I am terrible and stupid and you are all very disappointed in me," I said, "I got it already, thank you."

"Freddy," he said. "I just wanted to ask you why,"

he asked. "It's not like you to, well . . . honestly, to care about Maths enough to cheat."

"It's not my fault!" I shouted. "It's the New Girl, Aoife! She is always acting like she's the best and robots are rubbish, and I just wanted to **SHOW** her, and . . . and . . ."

"Oh my goodness," said Dad, and he grinned. "This . . . was to impress a girl?"

"**NO!**" I shouted angrily. Although I mean, yes, technically Aoife was a girl. And I suppose technically I was trying to impress her. But **GAAAHHH, NO,** not like **THAT!**

"It's just not FAIR!" I said. "Everyone's acting like I **CHEATED,** and it wasn't **CHEATING,** I was just using my natural abilities! I can't help it if my natural abilities are better than everyone else's!"

"That's not really the point, Freddy," said Dad. "It's about what's fair. Like, for example, say you had someone at your school whose family were really rich . . ."

"We do!" I said. "Malik, in the year above! He has **SIXTEEN CONSOLES!**"

"Right, well," continued Dad, "if Malik's family really are that rich . . ."

"SIXTEEN CONSOLES!" I shouted.

". . . then he could probably afford to pay someone to do his homework for him, right? But that wouldn't be fair, would it? It wouldn't be fair to the rest of you . . . but also, it wouldn't be fair to Malik. Because he wouldn't be learning anything. Do you see what I mean?"

"I think I do," I said. "Thanks, Dad."

And honestly I didn't **AT ALL**, but that was clearly what he wanted to hear, because it made him smile and go away and I got left in peace to have a nice daydream about paying people to do my homework for me and having **SIXTEEN CONSOLES.**

CHAPTER 9

Back at school the next day, the **TEAM HUMAN VS TEAM ROBOT** contest had turned into an actual **CRAZE**, like that week last year when everyone suddenly got super into swapping *Star Norse* cards. It seemed like the whole school was talking about it, arguing about who was going to win and getting in on the **BETTING**. When I went out on the playground at break, there was Henrik holding his little gambling book, talking to a squad of boys from Alex's year.

"Alright," said one of them, who seemed to be the boss. "Two family-size Chox and a bottle of Gunk on the girl to win."

Henrik started to write it down in his book, and then the boss gave him a shove.

"And she'd better win," he said.

And Henrik **GULPED**. Henrik, looking scared of someone! It was **VERY ENTERTAINING**.

Anyway, then the boss and his two mates wandered off across the playground, laughing and shouting **"TEAM HUMAN."** And then they spotted Alex coming the other way, and they all ran round him shouting **"TEAM HUMAN"** and donking him on the head, and

then ran off laughing. But Alex . . . definitely wasn't. He looked up, and saw me, and walked right over to me in the playground. And usually at school Alex has a pretty strict policy of Pretending I Do Not Exist, so I could tell something was up.

"This is all you, isn't it?" he asked. "Your dumb **CONTEST.**"

"How do you know about that?" I asked.

"Everyone's talking about it!" he said. "In class, at

break, it's all **TEAM HUMAN** this and **HUMANS VS ROBOTS** that. I'm **SICK** of it."

"Well, don't worry, because it'll all be over soon," I said, "when **I TOTALLY WIN**."

"And do you think that'll be the end of it?" asked Alex. "Or do you think then people will want a rematch, and another and another?"

"Well, then I'll just win **THEM!**" I shouted.

"My point is, you're making everyone — the whole school — pick sides."

"So **WHAT?**" I asked.

"Aaaargh!" shouted Alex, annoyed for some reason. "This is **TYPICAL** of you, Freddy. I've spent so long trying to go under the radar here — to avoid exactly this happening — and then you come in and blow it all up for a stupid **GAME**."

"It is **NOT** stupid," I shouted back. "And anyway, I am **TOTALLY GOING TO WIN!** And **PROVE** that robots are the best! You should be **HAPPY!**"

"**HAPPY?**" shouted Alex. "Do you know how many jokes and comments and **HILARIOUS** robot impressions I've had to listen to in the last couple of days?"

"So what?" I said. "Those guys are morons, who cares?"

And Alex just suddenly looked really tired. "Freddy," he said, "you don't get it. Listen to me. **US VERSUS THEM** is never a good idea, okay? For anyone."

"**YOU** don't get it," I argued back. "It's just a game! I don't know why you're being so weird about it!"

"You know what?" said Alex. "I give up. Do what you want. Just leave me out of it!"

And he stomped off across the playground.

"Fine!" I shouted after him. "I **WILL!** And anyway, Us Versus Them is a **GREAT** idea . . . as long as **US WINS!**"

And he didn't have a comeback to that, because he had gone.

Which meant that I . . .

CHAPTER 10

The next day, after lunch, we had our first P.E. lesson with the **Teacher-Bots**.

"This is going to be super boring, isn't it?" said Aoife, as we all walked out on to the field. "I bet it's all like . . ."

"BEEP!"

"Run back and forth in straight lines!"

And everyone laughed.

And then Henrik joined in . . .

"BEEP!"

"Do one
million
press-ups!"

And everyone laughed again, except Riyad who
went "Ulp!" and looked
worried, because Being
Forced To Do Press-Ups
is pretty much his worst
nightmare.

"It **MIGHT** be good,"
said Fernando.

"Yeah, I heard they have like tennis ball cannon
arms," said Anisha, "so they can fire lots of balls

at you, and you get to practise hitting them back. **THAT** would be cool."

"That is a lovely fantasy world you are living in, guys," said Aoife, "but no, let's face it, it's going to be rubbish."

And there was a general grumble of agreement, and I could see Aoife smirking.

"BEEP! Hey, guys, let's EXERCISE!"

"Today we will be doing some fun exercise to improve your **STAMINA** and **FITNESS!**"

. . . said the robot, when we all lined up on the side of the football pitch.

"Here we go . . ." said Aoife.

"BEEP!" said the robot. "FIRST, PLEASE RUN IN A STRAIGHT LINE TO THE OTHER END OF THE FOOTBALL PITCH AND BACK, TEN TIMES!"

And there was a general **GROAN**, and Aoife said "Told you."

"BEEP!" said the robot. "AND AFTER THAT, WE WILL BE DOING . . . PRESS-UPS!"

"Oh, **PLEASE NO**," said Riyad, looking like he was about to faint.

"Relax, everyone, we don't have to do anything this robot says. I've been looking up how these things work," said Aoife, casually walking up beside the **Teacher-Bot**, "and I've learned a few tricks. Who wants to see something cool?"

Aoife suddenly ducked round behind the **Teacher-Bot**, pressed a couple of buttons on its back and this panel popped open.

"BEEP!" said the **Teacher-Bot**. "PLEASE STEP AWAY FROM MY CONTROL PANEL! PLEASE COMMENCE RUNNING!"

"Just give me a sec . . ." said Aoife. And she pressed a couple of buttons on its control panel, and suddenly the **Teacher-Bot's** face went dim, and it slumped forward like it had gone to sleep.

"There you go," said Aoife. "I did a manual override on its control unit." And everyone laughed and cheered, and you could just tell Aoife was loving it.

"And then you do this . . ." she said, and pressed a couple more buttons, and suddenly the **Teacher-Bot's** face lit up and it stood up straight again.

"BEEP! VOICE COMMAND MODE ACTIVATED!" said the **Teacher-Bot**.

"Hey, teacher, dance like a chicken!" said Aoife.

"BEEP! COMMAND ACCEPTED!" said the **Teacher-Bot**. And sure enough it **DID**, it started to dance like a **CHICKEN**, right there, bobbing back and forth and flapping its arms and going

And everyone in the class started laughing like this was the single **FUNNIEST THING THEY HAD EVER SEEN**.

"Now spin round!" said Henrik, joining in. And the robot started spinning round on the spot, still flapping its arms like a chicken.

"Now bark like a dog!" Henrik yelled, and **OF COURSE** the stupid robot started going **"BEEP! WOOF WOOF!"** while it still did its stupid chicken dance.

And that was it, I'd had enough. "Alright, leave it alone!" I shouted, stepping in front of the **Teacher-Bot**.

"What's the problem?" asked Henrik. "It's **FUNNY.**"

"You guys are being **JERKS!**" I said.

"Freddy, it **IS** kind of funny," said Fernando. "It's not, y'know . . . a person, like you. It's just . . ."

"A dumb robot," said Aoife.

"Hey!" I shouted. "That is **OFFENSIVE.**"

"Freddy, nobody means you," said Fernando. "We just mean, y'know, other robots."

"You don't get it, do you?" I shouted. And looking at his face, I could tell he didn't. No one understood why I was so angry.

I mean to be honest, I didn't even really understand it, I just knew they were all being **VERY ANNOYING**.

"Alright," said Fernando, stepping between us. "Maybe that's enough for now. Let's all move on, yeah?"

But I . . .

. . . did not feel like moving on.

In class the next day, Miss Obasi wanted to have A Talk with us all.

"I've been hearing something about some games some of you are playing," she said, in Tutor Time that morning. "Games about . . . Robots Versus Humans?"

And we all looked super innocent and confused and made "no idea what you're talking about, miss" faces.

"Well, if anyone was playing something like that . . . I just wanted you to know that I don't think it sounds like a very good idea. That sounds like the kind of game where people's feelings could get hurt."

And she looked at me.

"But, miss," said Aoife, putting her hand up, "aren't you always complaining to Mr Javid about the Robo-Teachers? Aren't you and some of the other teachers even organising a protest?"

Miss Obasi looked annoyed. "That may be true, Aoife," she said, "but what's that got to do with anything?"

"Well," said Aoife, "isn't that like you're playing Robots Versus Humans, too?"

"Aoife," began Miss Obasi, "that's a workplace issue for me and Mr Javid to worry about. It doesn't mean that I think robots are bad or dangerous . . ."

"Oh," said Aoife. "It's just that I was walking past the office yesterday afternoon, and I was sure I heard you shouting at Mr Javid that the **Teacher-Bots** were BAD and DANGEROUS."

"I . . . might have some concerns about their safe and proper use in school," said Miss Obasi, looking a bit flustered, "but that's not the same thing at all . . ."

"Oh," said Aoife, looking super innocent. "It's just that it kind of sounded like the same thing."

"My point," said Miss Obasi, "is that I don't like the sound of these games, and I will be keeping a close eye on the playground at break times from now on to make sure there isn't anything like that going on. Alright?"

And she did. She was hovering round the edge of the field all through break, staring at us and sucking down decaf coffee with a suspicious expression.

So we couldn't do the Final Challenge yet, and everyone just played football at break instead. Everyone except me.

I don't actually play football all that much. Usually, me and my friends are busy at break times playing awesome games I have invented, like Invasion of the Zombies, or The Great Alien–Dinosaur War, or What If Cats Took Over The World, or whatever. But I am an **AWESOME ROBOT** WITH ACTUAL **SUPER-POWERS** so I am pretty sure if I **DID** play football, I would be **AMAZING** at it.

Aoife though, definitely is good at football. Even though she only started at our school this term she is **ALREADY** captain of the football team, and **ALSO ALREADY** has set the record for Most Goals Scored in a Single Game and blah blah blah **FINE**, she is **GOOD**, okay. So she was running round scoring goals and being in charge. They were all having a great time, all laughing and high-fiving and happily being Team Human together.

"Freddy!" Fernando shouted. "Come on. Join in!"

"**NO THANK YOU!**" I shouted back. "I am **QUITE BUSY**, actually."

"Busy sulking," I just heard Aoife say, and there was some laughter.

I was still really cross with them all, about the thing with the **Teacher-Bot** and the PE lesson. They were all being such jerks about it. I know they said they were making fun of the **Teacher-Bot**, not me. But it really felt like they were making fun of me. And none of them seemed to get it. Or to care.

At the end of break, a couple of kids from the year above were asking what had happened with the whole **TEAM HUMAN VS TEAM ROBOT** contest, because they'd already put bets on the final outcome.

"I mean . . . it's over, right?" said Riyad. "We can't finish it here, with Miss Obasi watching all the time, so we can just . . . call it a draw, and end there?"

"No!" said Henrik. "We can't stop now! I'd have to give everyone their Chox back!"

"And I still need to prove that Humans Are Better Than Robots," said Aoife.

"And I still need to prove the **EXACT OPPOSITE**," I said.

"Alright, alright, everyone calm down. I've had an idea," said Anisha. "For how we can do the final challenge. But I'll warn you now . . ."

And then she paused dramatically, and everyone leaned in . . .

". . . it's going to be **AWESOME**."

CHAPTER 12: THE FINAL CHALLENGE...

1	1

The final challenge was, it turned out, at the park after school. It is just a little playground and a couple of benches between our road and the flats. There's always loads of kids around and like half the families at our school live in flats looking out over it.

"Behold . . ." shouted Anisha . . .

THE TOWER OF TERROR

It is this BIG tall **CLIMBING FRAME** that you can kind of go up **DIFFERENT PATHS** inside, and you can't see where you're going, so **SOMETIMES** you'll get stuck up a **DEAD END**, or come **OUT** down an **UNEXPECTED SLIDE**.

"You have to start from the other side of the playground, then climb up through the tower. First one to the top claims the flag . . ." said Anisha, pointing to where Henrik had tied a T-shirt from someone's P.E. kit that we'd found in the Lost Property at school, which Anisha had written **FLAG** on in pen,

". . . and **WINS!**"

"That's it?" I said

"That's it," said Anisha.

And I couldn't quite believe it. Because this was **AMAZING** for me. Because Aoife is new here, and goes home the other way from school, I don't know if she'd even ever been to the park before. But I've been coming here for ever, and me and Fernando know every inch of that thing. We'd even given names to all the different bits inside it, and spent ages memorising the quickest route to the top. Which is . . . **UP** the Devil's Ladder, **THROUGH** the Mirror Tunnel **INTO** the second passage, **THROUGH** the maze and finally **OUT** on to the summit!

I looked over at Aoife, and she didn't look so smug this time. She looked all serious, almost like she was in a trance, just **STARING** at the tower like she was trying to figure it **OUT**.

"Oh, and there's a Secret Surprise Obstacle," said Anisha.

"What's that?" I said.

"It's a surprise!" said Anisha. "I'm trying to make it more exciting! It IS the final."

"Fine," said Aoife. "Let's do it."

"Okay! Contestants!" shouted Anisha, as we went and lined up by the swings. "Are you ready?"

"I am **READY**," I said.

"I am **READIER**," said Aoife, annoyingly.

"Okay!" said Anisha. "On your marks! Get set! And . . ."

GO!

We both **LAUNCHED** into action — Aoife setting off at a sprint, and me **ACTUALLY LAUNCHING**. **FWOOSH**! I fired off my **ROCKET BOOSTERS** and **FLEW** across the playground, straight towards the tower. I'd be there in seconds! This was going to be —

THWAKKK!!

Something hit me, right between the eyes, and I was so startled I **SWERVED** and flew straight into a **BIN**.

"What was **THAT**?" I shouted, picking myself up out of the bin and looking around.

"That was me!" shouted Henrik, grinning and waving a tennis racket, with a whole pile of balls at his feet. "I am being a Secret Surprise Obstacle!"

And then he hit another tennis ball into my face.

Aoife raced past me, heading straight for the tower.

"Well, hit some at her, then!" I shouted. And Henrik did a really half-hearted lob, sending a ball sailing gently past her.

"This is **TOTALLY UNFAIR!**" I shouted.

And then Henrik hit another tennis ball in my face.

"FREDDY!" shouted Fernando. "Just get **ON** with it! She's almost at the tower!"

And she was! So **FWOOOSSH**, I fired off my **ROCKET BOOSTERS** again and flew after her, dodging tennis balls as I went.

Aoife got to the tower just ahead of me and was first in. But I wasn't worried. Like I said, I knew every inch of this thing. I just had to wait for Aoife to take a wrong turn so I could nip past her and **WIN**.

But, the thing was, she didn't seem to be **MAKING** any wrong turns. She went **STRAIGHT UP** the Devil's Ladder, and then **THROUGH** the Mirror Tunnel, and then she got to the bit where there are the three passages you have to choose from. And I was **SURE** she'd go for the first one or the third one, but she just paused for a second . . .

And then went into the right one!

How was she doing this? She must be cheating. Someone must have told her! I was right behind her as we went into the tube maze, and I was just **WAITING** for her to slip up and take a wrong turn, but she never did!

. . . and before you knew it, we were nearly at the top, and if I didn't do something she was going to **WIN!** And then she'd do that **ANNOYING FACE** . . .

It was so unfair! How was everything so easy for her? How did she just magically know how to **DO** all this stuff?

And I must have just been feeling really **ANGRY** because before I even really knew what I was doing, I put my hand on the rail of the climbing frame . . .

. . . and **ZAPPED** it. Just sent a tiny little **ZAP** of static electricity into it. Not enough to hurt anyone! Just enough . . . to give someone a **TINY** little bit of a shock.

And it worked — Aoife went "Eep!" and stopped for a second like she was stunned . . .

. . . but a second was all I needed! I **FIRED** up my **ROCKET BOOSTERS** and FLEW past her and into the final tube, and clambered up it, and then **OUT!**

There was a **CHEER** from below as people saw me come out onto the top of the tower. I could see the "flag" fluttering, and I moved to go to grab it . . .

. . . but something was stopping me. Aoife was just coming out of the tunnel, and she had **GRABBED** hold of my trouser leg.

"Let go!" I shouted. "That's cheating!"

"**YOU** cheated!" she shouted back. "I don't know what you did, but you **MUST** have!"

"I didn't! Get **OFF** me!" I shouted.

"You **DID!** You **MUST** have!" Aoife said. And as she said it, gave my leg a big **YANK**.

"Hey!" I shouted, as I tried to reach for something to grab onto. "Stop it! You're going to–"

And then she gave it another big **YANK**, and my foot slipped off the side of the tower –

My head hit one of the bars
of the climbing frame,
and then . . .

WHACK!

It hit another
and then . . .

WHACK!

It hit several
more until
finally . . .

KRACKK!!!

CHAPTER 14

The next thing I remember is sort of waking up and opening my eyes and looking up and everything was blurry and Fernando was saying . . .

" . . . reddy? Freddy?"

And I sat up, rubbing my head.

"He's okay!" Fernando shouted.

And I was. I mean, I am **BASICALLY** indestructible. It's just, if I get a really **BIG** whack, like for, example, someone knocking me off the top of a giant **CLIMBING FRAME**, it can make me do a Forced Reboot, which feels a bit weird.

Everyone was chattering away, asking if I was okay and looking to see if my head was dented and stuff, and then suddenly everyone stopped chattering and went very quiet.

And I looked round and saw Aoife, climbing down off the tower. And **EVERYONE** was looking at her. And she was just staring at the ground.

And then the whispering started. And suddenly I realised, no one knew **WHY** she'd done it. They hadn't seen me do the static electricity zap. They'd just seen me about to win, and Aoife suddenly losing it and pushing me off the top.

Everyone looked to Anisha, and Anisha just gave Aoife a long look and then said . . .

"Judge's ruling! Aoife is disqualified. **FREDDY WINS**."

And the crowd **ERUPTED** with cheers! Everyone who'd bet on me at 2 to 1 started running up to Henrik to claim their winnings, and he looked all panicky and shouted "Look! Over there!" And then he straight up **RAN AWAY**, chased by an actual **MOB**. Aoife was just standing there, looking shocked. "No, it's not . . ." she started to say. "You don't get it, he . . ."

And Anisha just looked at her coldly and said, "Judge's ruling is **FINAL**."

And some of the people who were left started booing and hissing Aoife. And I couldn't really tell if she was angry or sad, but her bottom lip started to go, and then she ran away too, with everyone still booing and hissing.

People were laughing and clapping me on the back. And I realised, it was over! The final score was officially . . .

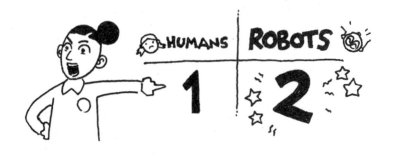

. . . and that meant I'd won the whole thing!

So I looked around for my friends, to celebrate. But Riyad wasn't there, he'd wandered off. And Anisha had gone too. And Henrik had been chased away by angry gamblers. I was surrounded by a crowd of randos. And my head felt kind of weird from the Forced Reboot.

Fernando was still there, at least. I think he could tell I was feeling a bit wobbly, because he put his arm round my shoulders and said, "Come on. I got you."

And we set off out the back of the park and across the little alley behind the shops, back to my road. It felt like something was up, because Fernando was not laughing or celebrating, but looked **WEIRDLY SERIOUS**.

"What's up?" I asked him. "We **WON!**"

"Yeah, but Freddy . . ." he said. And now he had a look on his face so serious it was starting to worry me. "I was sitting at the bottom of the tower. I could see right up into the tunnels."

"Um, so?" I said, getting a bad feeling about this.

"So I **SAW** you," said Fernando. "I saw you **CHEAT.**"

"What do you mean?" I asked. "I didn't cheat!"

"Freddy, come on," said Fernando. "I was right there, I saw you."

"**WHAT** did you see?" I asked. Thinking that maybe he hadn't seen the whole thing, and there might still be a chance for me to **DENY EVERYTHING**.

"Well," said Fernando, "I saw you touch the rail and fire off one of your **ELECTRIC ZAPS**, and then Aoife got shocked and fell down, and you used your **ROCKET BOOSTERS** and flew past her to win."

Alright, so apparently he **HAD** seen the whole thing.

"Okay, but look," I said. "I didn't even **MEAN** to, really. I just got really angry and it sort of came out. And I didn't **HURT** her, she just got . . . a tiny bit stunned."

"Freddy, the rule was **NO USING YOUR POWERS AGAINST AOIFE**. That was literally the One Rule. And you electrocuted her!"

"I only electrocuted her a **TINY BIT!**" I protested. "I can't believe **YOU** are hassling me about this. Like, there is a sign on the wall of the school telling me not to use my **ROCKET BOOSTERS** and stuff, and **YOU** are the one who's always trying to get me to ignore it!"

"Yeah, but those are stupid school rules. This was an us rule. It's different."

And it **WAS** different, and I **KNEW** it was different, and that was starting to make me feel bad. And I really **DID NOT LIKE** that.

"Look," I said. "I **HAD** to do it. Aoife was going to win. And then she would have proved Humans Are Better Than Robots! I couldn't let that happen! You know she'd never stop going on about it. It's Aoife. She is terrible!"

"She **IS** terrible," Fernando agreed. "She is bossy, and thinks she knows everything, and is always showing off . . ."

"So you agree!" I said.

". . . but she doesn't **CHEAT**," said Fernando. "And now everyone thinks she's a **TERRIBLE MONSTER** for knocking you off the tower and they don't know **WHY**. That's just . . . not okay, Freddy."

And now I felt **REALLY** bad. And that made me **REALLY** angry.

"Why are you taking her side?" I asked. "Oh wait, I know! **BECAUSE SHE IS A HUMAN.**"

"Oh, for . . ." said Fernando.

"I see how it is!" I shouted. "You all like me when I'm blowing things up with *LASERS* or giving you rocket piggybacks. But when it comes down to it you'll always side with each **OTHER.**"

"You are being very stupid," said Fernando.

"Oh, because I am a robot? Just a **STUPID ROBOT?**"

"I didn't say that!" said Fernando. "But actually, yes!

You **ARE** a robot, and you are being **VERY STUPID**. So technically **YES**, you are a **STUPID ROBOT!**"

"Yeah, well you are a **STUPID HUMAN!**" I yelled. "And you are **BANISHED FROM TEAM ROBOT** FOREVER!"

"Fine!" Fernando shouted.

"Fine!" I agreed.

"FINE!" Fernando agreed again.

Anyway, while we had been arguing we'd made it as far back as my house, so Fernando just left me there at the doorstep and stomped off back up the road.

Stupid Fernando. Trying to make me feel bad about Aoife. **AOIFE**. Like I should feel bad about **HER!**

Which of course, **I TOTALLY DID NOT**.

AT ALL.

DEFINITELY.

CHAPTER 16

When I got home, Mum had seen me and Fernando arguing on the doorstep. But **LUCKILY**, she had no idea what it was all about, and I wasn't about to tell her. She kept asking me what was wrong, but I just went "nothing" a lot until finally she gave up.

"Fine," said Mum. "Don't tell me anything. But whatever it is, for goodness' sake try and sort it out. What's the alternative, you just sit around the house all weekend **SULKING?**"

So . . . I sat around the house all weekend. But I wasn't **SULKING**. I was just **ANGRY** with everyone else for being **JERKS!** There is a **BIG DIFFERENCE!**

So I was **TRYING** to play a nice game of Streets of Fighting 2: **CHAINSAW PARTY**, but people kept interrupting and asking dumb questions like "what's wrong?" and "what's got into you?" and "what are you sitting there sulking about?"

"I'm not **SULKING!**" I shouted, after Alex had come in and asked me that last one, for like the 100th time. So I threw the controller at his head, and then shot him with lasers, and then we had a bit of a fight.

Later, when we had finished **PUNCHING** and **SHOOTING** each other with **LASERS**, he asked me again, "Seriously though, what is it?"

"Oh **FINE**," I said. "So here's the thing. Say that **MAYBE** you had done something wrong. And, **ALSO MAAYBE**, someone else was getting the blame. And, **STILL COMPLETELY MAAAAYBE**, you knew that they were feeling bad. And that was making **YOU** feel bad. And you just wanted to stop feeling bad. What would you do?"

"Just . . . stop being an idiot, is what I'd do," he said, "in your **OBVIOUSLY TOTALLY MADE-UP** situation. If I knew that someone else was feeling bad because of something I'd done . . . I'd go and apologise."

"Ugh, do I have to?" I asked.

"Yes! You are sorry — that's why you're feeling bad. So just **SAY** sorry. They'll feel better for hearing it, you'll feel better for saying it. It's not complicated."

Ugh, I thought. Saying sorry. And to Aoife. This was going to be awful.

"I bet she totally milks it . . ." I muttered.

"She?" said Alex, who suddenly got a **REALLY ANNOYING** expression on his face. "Freddy . . . is this about a **GIRL**?"

And then I shot him with **LASERS** again.

So it was later that afternoon. Anisha had showed me where Aoife lives, and it was actually right round the corner, in the block of flats just behind our house. So I clenched my fists, and walked up the stairwell to her door, and braced myself to do the most unpleasant and horrifying thing I could ever imagine.

Say sorry.

I knocked, and I heard big, heavy steps coming towards the door. And then it swung open, and . . .

. . . it wasn't Aoife.

It was a man, big and tall and generally **MASSIVE**. I guess he was her dad? And he looked all tired and confused and **ANNOYED**, like he had just been in the middle of something. And then he peered down at me, and looked even **MORE** confused and annoyed.

"Eh? What is it?" he yelled at me. Like, proper **YELLED**.

"Um, hello," I said. "Is—"

"No, no, we don't want any. Clear off," he said.

"I just—"

And then he said a **PROPER SWEAR**, and ". . . can't you **READ**? Your **LANGUAGE RECOGNITION**

CIRCUITS not working?" And he pointed to this sign taped up next to their doorbell which, OK, I totally hadn't noticed. It said:

"I'm not . . ." I tried to say. "I just . . ."

"I SAID, we don't want any. BLOODY things!" he said. And he SLAMMED the door in my FACE! And I was so shocked that I kind of staggered backwards, and tripped over my own feet and FELL down the starwell, and . . .

WHACK!!

I hit my head on one of the steps,

. . . and then

WHACK! WHACK! WHACK!

. . . on several **MORE** on the way down . . .

. . . until I came to rest on the landing.

I just lay there rebooting on the landing for a second, with no idea what had just happened. My first instinct was to fly right back up there and blow everything up with lasers, but you're not supposed to do that with People's Dads. But People's Dads aren't supposed to slam **DOORS** in your face either. And suddenly I just felt really confused, and embarrassed, and I didn't even know why, but I felt like I was going to start crying.

I picked myself up and ran down the rest of the stairs and back out the front door of the flats. I didn't care about saying sorry to Aoife any more, I didn't care about any of it, I just wanted to get **HOME**.

And then I heard this **KNOCK! KNOCK!**

And I looked up, and there, in the window of one of the flats, banging on the glass, I could see . . .

Aoife.

I used my Optical Zoom to **ZOOM** in on her face. And she looked . . . Different from usual. She wasn't smirking or sneering. She looked worried, and sad.

She waved at me, and then she made a "come on up" gesture.

I looked back at the door — there was no way I was going back up those stairs. I looked back at Aoife, and she made the "come up" gesture again. And so . . .

I looked around, and then I fired up my **ROCKET BOOSTERS** . . .

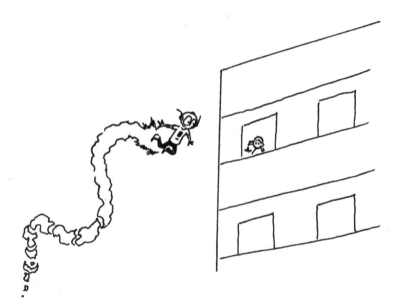

And I **FLEW** up there.

CHAPTER 18

Aoife opened up her bedroom window and I **FLEW** through it. I was trying to be careful, but I accidentally knocked a book over and it landed with a **THUMP**. Aoife grabbed me and pulled me close and whispered "**SSSH**. My **DAD'll** hear . . ."

And, y'know, I was **NOT** in a hurry to meet that guy again. So I tried to be careful. It was hard **NOT** to kick a book over though, because there were literally books everywhere. On shelves, and piled up on **TOP** of shelves, and on the floor **BESIDE** the shelves, and all over a little desk in the corner and, well, like I say, everywhere.

I guess Aoife likes to **READ**.

"What are you doing here, Freddy?" said Aoife. "I was in the middle of my Maths homework."

"I was just, um, in the neighbourhood . . ." I said, feeling a bit embarrassed. And then I suddenly thought of something.

"Wait a minute," I said, "**WHAT** Maths homework? We don't have any Maths homework."

And we didn't, I was sure about that. Because when we get given Maths homework I always spend a good hour complaining about it and daydreaming about blowing things up with *LASERS*, and I hadn't done that today.

"Yeah, um . . . you wouldn't, it's . . . look, I always ask Miss Obasi to give me extra Maths home-work," she said. And she looked a bit embarrassed, and I could understand why, because that was the **CRAZIEST THING** I ever **HEARD**.

"You **ASK?** For **EXTRA? MATHS HOMEWORK?**" I said.

"I'm not **CRAZY**," she said, apparently reading my mind. "I just . . . I've always found Maths really hard, so I ask for extra homework to help me get the hang of it."

"What? You're really good at Maths! You are like the **BEST!** Um, apparently," I said, suddenly thinking about the Second Challenge.

"Yeah . . . because of all the extra homework," she said slowly, looking at me like I was a bit simple.

"Huh," I said. And I looked at her little desk in the corner there and, sure enough, there were Maths books all piled up on it. And above the desk, Blu-Tacked to the wall, there was a big sheet of paper with this weird **DIAGRAM** thing on it. I couldn't figure it out at ALL. There were hundreds of neatly ruled lines in every colour pen imaginable, so incredibly complicated it looked like someone was trying to design a robotic insect or possibly

DESTROY THE WORLD??

"What is **THAT?**" I asked.

"Um," said Aoife, looking embarrassed again. "It's my Extra-Curricular Timetable."

And then I could suddenly see it. It was our timetable from school in the middle, showing what classes we have when, just like everyone has. But then around it and on top of it there was all this **EXTRA** stuff, drawn by hand in a whole rainbow explosion of different coloured pens and neatly ruled lines. There was lots of **MATHS PRACTICE** in red pen and **EXTRA SWIMMING** in orange, and one in yellow that was hard to read but I think said **"FOOTBALL CLUB"**, and Science Clubs and Computing Clubs and Hockey Clubs and Karate Clubs. It was the most complicated thing I have ever seen in my life.

I would hate for Aoife to see **MY** Extra-Curricular Timetable, because (A) I don't have one, and (B) if I did it would pretty much just say . . .

I guess I was still staring at the timetable, because Aoife suddenly said "I'm not weird, you know. I just . . . hate being bad at stuff."

"I didn't say you were weird" I said. Although, **YES**, obviously I had been thinking it.

"My dad always says we've got to be the best we can be," she said. "Make it as hard as possible for them to replace us."

"Them? Who?" I asked, turning to look at Aoife. "What do you . . ."

And then I stopped.

Because I'd just caught a proper glimpse inside her cupboard. And what was in there . . .

. . . was the coolest thing I have ever seen in my entire life.

So, in case you didn't know:

STAR NORSE

. . . is this TV show about a bunch of Norse gods who live in **SPACE** and are always having epic adventures and fighting Ice Giants and World Dragons and stuff, but also **ARE GIANT ROBOTS**.

It is, basically, the greatest thing ever. And there, on shelf after shelf, inside Aoife's cupboard . . .

. . . was literally every *Star Norse* toy **EVER MADE**.

"What the . . .?" I said, articulately. "How the . . .? **WHAT THE** . . .?"

"Oh," said Aoife, "yeah. That's my collection."

"You . . . have . . . **SO MANY!**" I said. And I was actually slightly in **AWE**. "You have Thorr-Tron! And Super God Mode Thorr-Tron! And Ultimate Super Maximum DoubleGodPlus Mode Thorr-Tron! And . . . I don't even know what this one is!"

"That is Ragnarök Final Battle Mode Thorr-Tron," said Aoife, taking it down off the shelf. "Look, he has Authentic Battle Damage from fighting the World Dragon."

"I never even **HEARD** of this one," I said, slightly in awe.

"Yeah," said Aoife. "It was a limited edition. They only made like a hundred."

"So how did . . . how come you . . ." I started to say. And then I got it.

"Wait," I said. "Are you like **SUPER RICH?**"

Of course she was. She must be. It explained everything. No wonder she was so good at everything, she must have had **PRIVATE LESSONS** and **TUTORS** and **FANCY EXPENSIVE SCHOOLS**. And she got all the *Star Norse* toys in the world as well, because some people just get **EVERYTHING**, I guess.

"I'm not rich," she said. "My dad . . . he used to work at the place where they made these. He was a designer."

"Oh cool!" I said. And then I thought, that guy? What happened?

"But then he lost his job," she said. "Got laid off. They automated the whole place. He got replaced . . ."

"Oh," I said. And I thought, I know what's coming next.

". . . by a robot," Aoife said.

And I thought, there it is.

"It wasn't me," I said, feeling weirdly defensive.

"I didn't say it was," said Aoife, also sounding weirdly defensive.

She picked up a Super God Mode Loki-Bot from the shelf and started playing with it absent-mindedly.

"They have these design-bots now that just run an algorithm and boop, out pop new designs. Anyway, ever since then . . . he's been in a bit of a mood."

And I suddenly felt the weirdest thing. Like I just wanted to stay there, in Aoife's room, with her. Just hanging out and talking and playing **AWESOME STAR NORSE GAMES**.

"Listen," I said "I came round . . . to say sorry. About the contest thing . . ."

And suddenly everything got even **MORE** confusing, because Aoife grabbed my **HAND** and was holding my **HAND**.

"I'm sorry!" She said. "I pushed you! I . . . I was so angry, I just lost it. I'm just glad you're okay!"

"I'm fine," I said. "I am basically indestructible." Not to

show off, but um, also possibly slightly to show off.

"I know I get too competitive," Aoife said. "With the contest, the whole thing. I just . . . it's hard, starting at a new school and not knowing anyone. It was just . . . it was like fitting in was a problem to solve, and the only way I know how to solve problems is just to go at them super hard . . ." Aoife paused for a second looking a bit embarrassed. "There on top of the climbing frame – I was so sure I was about to win, and then I saw you there ahead of me and I just . . . I thought you must have cheated, and I just lost it."

"Well. Um. That's the thing," I said. "It's funny. I didn't **CHEAT** exactly, but I might have accidentally given off a **TINY** little, um, static electric shock . . ."

And suddenly, Aoife pulled her hand away.

And suddenly she looked really **REALLY** cross.

"I knew it!" she said. "I **KNEW** it. You **CHEATED!**"

"It wasn't cheating!" I said, confused. "I was just . . . using my natural abilities!"

"You totally cheated and you **KNOW** it! Ugh! I **FELT** something, I should have **KNOWN**. I can't believe I was feeling **BAD** for a . . ."

"For a what?" I said. And I was suddenly feeling really angry and upset, like I had actually started to think she was okay, and now **THIS**.

"For a **STUPID ROBOT!**" she said, and **THREW** the Loki-Bot, and it bounced off my head and crashed into the wall with a **WHACK!**"

"Aoife?" came a voice from down the hall. "What's going on in there? You're supposed to be doing your homework."

"Go!" whispered Aoife, suddenly looking completely panicked. "If he finds you here he'll . . . look, just **GO!**"

"I'm not scared of you, and I'm not scared of your dumb dad," I said.

And then . . .

Aoife **SLAPPED** me across the face. And she hissed at me, "Just **GO**."

So I did. I ***BLASTED OFF***, sending maths books and papers flying everywhere, and ***ZOOMED*** out the window, and ***FLEW*** back down to the street. And then I landed, because I couldn't really see where I was going, because suddenly my eyes must have been malfunctioning or something.

Not crying. **MALFUNCTIONING**.

I just want to make sure that is clear.

In assemby the next day, Mr Javid had another **ANNOUNCEMENT**.

"Due to the **ENORMOUS SUCCESS** of our early trials in using Educational Support Robots . . ." he began, gesturing at a couple of the **Teacher-Bots** that he had up on stage with him, "I am excited to announce that commencing this week, we will be expanding the programme across all your classes."

And everyone looked at each other like, what is he talking about, "huge success", these things are **HOT GARBAGE.**

But Fernando whispered ". . . they're a **SUCCESS** because they mean he doesn't have to pay actual teachers' salaries any more, and he can spend it all on **FANCY CARS.**"

And it was true, Mr Javid did seem to keep turning up at school in fancier and fancier cars.

Anyway, apparently Fernando wasn't the only one who thought this, because suddenly Miss Obasi stood up, looking **FURIOUS.** And this time she didn't just storm out, she gave a look to the four or five other Actual Human Teachers who were still left, and they all got up and stormed out **WITH** her.

There was lots of **COMMOTION**; suddenly everyone was **WHISPERING** and also **TALKING** and also quite soon **SHOUTING**. Mr Javid looked all flustered and yelled, "Quiet! Everyone, quiet! Assembly cancelled! There will now be an extra ten minute break time, then please report to your Educational Support Robots for your next lessons!"

So we all went back out to the playground. Everyone was all excited and in a weird mood already, and when I got out there, I saw Aoife, standing in the middle of a big crowd of people, already playing it up.

". . . see?" she was saying. "It's exactly like I said. Taking jobs from real people." And there was a general **MURMUR** of agreement.

"Miss Obasi was a good teacher," she continued, and again there was a **MURMUR**, because she **WAS**. "And now she's gone. Just so they can save money by replacing people with these robots. These robots which are, let's be honest, complete rubbish."

"**IF** they're rubbish it's because **YOU** messed them all up!" I said.

"Well, they were pretty easy to mess up, weren't

they?" said Aoife. "Which totally proves it: humans are better than robots!"

"You are not allowed to say that!" I shouted. "We literally had a whole contest to decide who was best, and I **WON!**"

"Yeah, because you **CHEATED!**" shouted back Aoife.

And everyone went **OOOOOOHHHHHH**.

"Yeah!" said Henrik. "So I don't have to give everyone their chocolate bars back!"

"Give it up, Henrik," said Fernando. "Everyone **KNOWS** you already ate them all."

And everyone went **OOOOOOHHHHH** again.

"What we **OUGHT** to do," said Aoife, "is have a **REMATCH**. Settle it once and for all."

And there was a general **GRUMBLING** and **MUTTERING**, and people started to yell "**REMATCH! REMATCH!**"

"What do you say?" asked Aoife. "Let's have a **FINAL** Final Challenge. IF you're brave enough to give it a try without **CHEATING** this time?"

"Bring it on!" I shouted. "I will beat you at literally anything!"

"Fine," said Aoife, smiling. "Because I've got the perfect idea . . ."

. . . yelled Henrik. **"HUMANS VERSUS ROBOTS!**
Place your bets now!"

We were all in the gym, in our P.E. kits. And
everything felt super weird, because there weren't
any teachers around. Miss Obasi had led them

all off to organise a **PROTEST**, so we had one of the **Teacher-Bots** in charge, but it was just spinning round slowly in the corner and making chicken noises. It all felt a bit . . . on edge, like things were getting out of control. And now it was time for the **FINAL** Final Challenge. Which was going to be . . .

Football.

"Okay!" I shouted. "Let's do this! Who's going to be on **TEAM ROBOT**? Let's crush these stupid humans!"

And I looked at Riyad. But he didn't come over to me. And I looked at Fernando. But he didn't come over to me either.

"Anisha?" I said, hopefully, because she is super good at football.

"I'm the referee," said Anisha. "I have to be impartial."

"Oh yeah, right!" I said, feeling really annoyed. "If you're so impartial, why are you always taking her side?"

"I'm not!" said Anisha, looking offended.

"You **TOTALLY** are! You've been on her side the whole time! It is a **CONSPIRACY** of **GIRLS!**"

"Freddy," said Anisha, looking deeply annoyed, "I have been doing my best to be impartial this whole time. And it has not been easy, because you have been being a **COMPLETE IDIOT.**"

"See?!" I shouted. **"NOT IMPARTIAL!"**

"You know what, Freddy?" said Anisha. "Fine. If that's how you want to be, I might as **WELL** be on her team."

And she walked over and stood next to Aoife on Team Human.

"That's it!" I shouted at Anisha. "You are officially **BANISHED FROM TEAM ROBOT FOREVER!**"

"Freddy," said Fernando, "there **IS** no Team Robot. You already kicked everyone **OUT**."

And Fernando went and stood next to Anisha in Team Human. And I looked at Riyad, who just looked really stressed out, but went and stood with them too.

"When was the last time we did anything **FUN?**" asked Fernando. "It's not fun any more, it's just . . ."

". . . you telling us that you're better than us," said Riyad quietly.

"Talking about stupid humans," muttered Fernando.

"Over and over and **OVER**," said Anisha.

"But I . . . but . . ." I began. "I didn't mean you. I meant, you know . . . other humans."

But it was too late. They were all standing next to Aoife, who was looking **SUPER SMUG**. She'd won already, they were all on Team Human now, and I was all on my own.

"Fine!" I shouted. "I don't care, I'll beat you all anyway! I am an **AWESOME ROBOT** and you are just a **BUNCH** of **JERKS!**"

"Um," said Riyad. "Maybe we should just call the whole thing off?"

"NO!!!" shouted Aoife, and Henrik, and Fernando, and Anisha, and me.

"But . . . Freddy hasn't got anyone to be on his team," said Riyad. "You can't play football five-against-one, it's not fair."

"Oh, I know who can be on his team . . ." said Aoife.

And she walked over to the Storage Cupboard off the side of the gym, where they keep all the sports equipment.

"I watched Mr Latif do this and learned the combination," she said, pressing buttons on the door's keypad. "This should be . . ."

And the doors sprang open. The inside of the Storage

Cupboard was dark. There were big bags of footballs and basketballs and netball balls. And also, weirdly, a couple of empty cans of Gunk, this super sweet sticky fizzy drink we're not supposed to have in school, lying on the floor. (Maybe Mr Latif used to sneak in here to feed his **SECRET GUNK HABIT?**)

And at the back of the cupboard, standing there silently in the darkness, were . . .

"There you go," said Aoife. "There's your team."

Of course.

CHAPTER

It was **ON**. We all lined up in the gym.

One one side you had . . .

Fernando, Anisha, Aoife, Riyad, and Henrik in goal. Which seemed unfair as he basically **FILLED** the goal, but anyway.

On the other side there was . . .

ME, and . . . four of the **Teacher-Bots**.

I guess Aoife thought she was being pretty funny, putting me on a team with all the **Teacher-Bots**. But the joke was on her. Because I had an idea. To use Aoife's **OWN TRICKS** against her, and turn these guys into the most **UNSTOPPABLE FOOTBALL TEAM EVER!**

I went up to them and pressed the two buttons on their back units, like I'd seen Aoife do, and they all stood up straight and said, "SETTINGS OVERRIDE!

And then I pressed a couple more buttons, until they said, "BEEP! VOICE COMMAND MODE ACTIVATED!"

"I need you guys to PLAY **HARDER!**" I said. "Like, turn your **COMPETITIVENESS** setting to maximum."

"COMMAND ACKNOWLEDGED," they said. "**NEW COMPETITIVENESS SETTING: 100%.**"

"No, I need it **EVEN HIGHER!**" I said. "This is serious! I need you to . . . turn it up to 11! Give it one hundred and **TEN** percent!"

And the robots started saying "**LOGICAL ERROR**"

and making strange fizzing noises, but then they said, **"NEW COMPETITIVENESS SETTING: 110%."**

"One **THOUSAND** percent!" I shouted.

And they made even more weird noises, like cogs **GRINDING** against **GLASS**, but then they said **"NEW . . . COMPETITIVENESS . . . SETTING: 1,000%."**
"Good! That's better!" I said, pointing at Team Human

up the pitch. "See those guys? They are the **ENEMY**."

"THEY ARE THE ENEMY," repeated the **Teacher-Bots**.

"It's US and **THEM!**" I continued. "If you're not WITH us you're AGAINST us!"

"US AND THEM!" they all repeated. "NOT WITH US, AGAINST US!"

"I want you to BEAT them. CRUSH them. ANNIHILATE them," I said, really getting into my pep talk.

"BEAT THEM . . . CRUSH THEM . . . ANNIHILATE THEM . . ." repeated the **Teacher-Bots**.

"NOW you're getting it," I said.

"Hey!" shouted Aoife, from up the pitch. "Get a move on!"

"You see her?" I said to the **Teacher-Bots**, "She is the ENEMY CAPTAIN. She is your PRIMARY TARGET."

"BEEP!" said the **Teacher-Bots**. "PRIMARY TARGET IDENTIFIED."

"Are you ready for us to totally beat you yet?" called Aoife, from up the pitch. "We haven't got all day."

"Oh, we're ready," I said, **RUBBING MY HANDS TOGETHER** and **CACKLING**. But, y'know, quietly.

"Okay!" shouted Arjun from the year above, who had been drafted in as Temporary Replacement Referee. "Humans Versus Robots! Sudden Death rules — first team to three goals **WINS!** Ready . . ."

And he blew his whistle, and we were off!

I **PASSED** the ball to **Teacher-Bot 1**, and . . .

. . . and well, apparently my pep talk had **WORKED**, because it took off like someone had lit a **ROCKET** under it. It **RACED** up the centre of the pitch, straight past a suddenly very confused-looking Aoife and Fernando, paused for a second and said "**BEEP! TARGETING** . . ."

. . . and then **POWWWW**, it **FIRED** the ball straight up the pitch, and straight past Henrik and into the net before he had a chance to even figure out what was **HAPPENING**.

"GOAL!" shouted Arjun. "ROBOTS 1, HUMANS 0."

It was great! I didn't even have to do anything myself! We were winning, and Aoife was looking CONFUSED and ANNOYED in a way I found HIGHLY SATISFYING.

Aoife's team kicked off again, but this time Aoife had barely got the ball two feet up the pitch before **Teacher-Bot 3** ZOOMED past her so fast she didn't even SEE it, she just looked down at her feet and the ball was GONE.

The **Teacher-Bot** was just a blur! It ran STRAIGHT past Fernando, and Anisha, and an absolutely terrified-looking Riyad, and then . . .

"BEEP! TARGETING . . ."

It FIRED the ball into the goal, dead-on, so hard it KNOCKED Henrik off his feet and sent him FLYING.

"G . . . goal!" said Arjun, sounding a little worried. "Robots 2, Humans 0?"

"CRUSH THEM!" said **Teacher-Bot 3**.

"DESTROY THEM!" said **Teacher-Bot 4**.

"YEAH!" I said.
Aoife kicked off again — and this time she was

ready and she **JUST** managed to pull the ball out of the way of another super-fast **Teacher-Bot** tackle. Almost instantly, it spun round and was coming back for another try, so she **PUNTED** the ball up the pitch towards . . .

. . . Fernando, who was running forward to intercept it

But suddenly **Teacher-Bot 2** BARGED into him, knocking him to the ground.

Arjun's whistle blew, and Aoife and Anisha were yelling, "Foul!"

I ran over to Fernando to help him up, and he was okay, he just needed to check the fixings on his prosthetic leg. And then I looked up at **Teacher-Bot 2** and said "Not cool! Too much, okay?"

But **Teacher-Bot 2** was just standing there, shaking weirdly. And its screen kept glitching, and I swear there was actual **SMOKE** coming out of its ears, and it kept saying

"LOGICAL ERROR +++ LOGICAL ERROR +++"

"Um," said Fernando. "Freddy, your robot mate's gone weird."

"Yeah," I said, getting a bad feeling.

And then **Teacher-Bot 2** stood up straight. And **KA-CHING**, its cricket bat arms popped out of its side, and it started spinning them around like a maniac, yelling:

"THEY ARE THE ENEMY. CRUSH THEM. DESTROY THEM. ANNIHILATE!!!"

CHAPTER 23

2 0

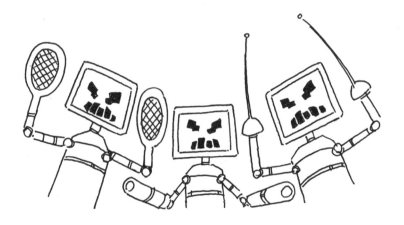

The score was 2-0. Team Robot only needed one more goal to WIN. And all the **Teacher-Bots** on my team had picked this moment . . . **TO GO COMPLETELY INSANE**. All their screens were glitching and smoke was pouring out of their heads and they were all deploying their Extra Sporting Attachments like **WEAPONS**.

KA-CHUNK! **Teacher-Bot 3** popped out a couple of tennis racket arms.

KA-CHOW! **Teacher-Bot 4** popped out TENNIS BALL CANNONS!

KA-CHINGGG! **Teacher-Bot 1** popped out a couple of swords! Like, **ACTUAL SWORDS**. Seriously, who **DESIGNED** these things and what school were **THEY** going to?

"CRUSH THEM! DESTROY THEM! ANNIHILATE THEM!" they yelled, **CHARGING** towards my friends.

"AAAAH!" yelled Riyad. "Run away!!"

And everyone **DID**. All the onlookers started **PANICKING** and running out of the gym screaming.

And Riyad and Henrik and Anisha were running for it too, but the **Teacher-Bots** were gaining on them . . .

"CRUSH THEM! DESTROY THEM! ANNIHILATE THEM!" yelled the **Teacher-Bots**, catching up with them.

"Aaah!" shouted Henrik, as ***POW POW POW POW POW***, a **Teacher-Bot** fired lots of tennis balls at his head like a machine gun. Which, okay, I admit, totally made me laugh.

"AAAAH!" yelled Riyad, as another **Teacher-Bot** advanced on him, swinging its Cricket Bat Arms menacingly. "I am going to die! In P.E.! **I ALWAYS KNEW ONE DAY THIS WOULD HAPPEN!**"

I had to save them!
I fired up my **ROCKET BOOSTERS** and
yelled . . .

MEGA ROBO POWER UP!!

. . . and I flew into the **Teacher-Bots** like a BOWLING BALL, sending them flying in all directions!

But only for a second! Straight away the **Teacher-Bots** were picking themselves up and advancing again.

"What's got into them?" asked Anisha.

"They're just trying to **WIN!**" I said. "I'm sorry! I just told them to be competitive!"

"They shouldn't ever be like **THIS** though," said Riyad, looking thoughtful and suddenly being much less panicky now he had an Interesting Science Problem to think about. "It's like all their Safety Circuits have been disabled, or . . ."

And then we heard a **SCREAM** from up the pitch. "Look!" shouted Fernando, pointing.

One of the **Teacher-Bots** had Aoife backed into the corner of the gym and was advancing towards her, shouting "BEEP! CRUSH! DESTROY! ANNIHILATE!"

And of course . . . it was the one with the **SWORDS**.

FWOOSSHHH, I ***FLEW*** straight for it at Mega Robo Super Speed, and ***POWWW***, I ***PUNCHED*** it so it flew back up the pitch, away from Aoife.

But straight away it started picking itself **UP** again, its eyes locked on to Aoife.

"BEEP!" it said. "**PRIMARY TARGET IDENTIFIED! ANNIHILATE!**"

And they **ALL** started ***ZOOMING*** towards us.

"They're after Aoife!" shouted Riyad. "She's the

CAPTAIN, so they're trying to get **HER!**"

"Then we need to get her out of here," I said. "Hold on . . ."

And . . .

FWOOSH! I held on to Aoife and *FLEW*, straight across the gym and into the Storage Cupboard, which seemed like the nearest safe place to go. I slammed the doors behind us and started barricading them shut with hockey sticks.

KRASH! THUD! WHACK! I could

hear the **Teacher-Bots** hammering on the door already. I didn't think the hockey sticks were going to hold long.

And then, from the darkness of the storage cupboard, I heard the weirdest sound I think I've ever heard in my life.

Aoife . . . was actually crying.

"I'm sorry," she said. "It's all my fault."

And I saw she'd picked up one of the empty gunk cans and was staring at it.

"I didn't mean for it to go this far . . ." she said.

"Aoife," I said, and suddenly I was getting **ANOTHER** Very Bad Feeling.

"What did you **DO?**"

CHAPTER 24

And right there in the Storage Cupboard, with the crazy rampaging **Teacher-Bots** hammering on the door to get in and **MURDER** us . . . Aoife confessed.

Looking totally pale, she told me . . . how before the lesson she'd sneaked into the Storage Cupboard with a couple of cans of Gunk, and then opened up the **Teacher-Bots**' Central Processor Units . . . and **POURED THE GUNK INSIDE**.

Wow, I thought. I guess my mum was right, that stuff really will melt your circuits.

"I just wanted to make them malfunction," Aoife sniffed, "go a bit weird . . ."

"Congratulations!" I said, as the door thudded and shook and the hockey sticks holding it shut started to splinter. "I think you achieved that."

"It must have corroded their Safety Circuits. I'm **SORRY!**" she said. "I was just trying to make them look stupid. I didn't know they'd go all . . . **MURDER-y!**"

And I thought about how I'd . . .

★ turned the **Teacher-Bots** up to 11

★ told them it was Us and Them

★ yelled at them to **CRUSH** and **DESTROY** and **ANNIHILATE THE HUMANS**.

"Look," I said. "Let's just agree it's nobody's fault."

And then there was another **THUD**. But this one wasn't coming from the doors . . .

Halfway up the wall at the back of the storage

room there was like a big **VENT** and suddenly it was **THUDDING** and **BANGING**.

"It's them!" I said. "They've found another way in!" And without thinking about it I tried to put my arm in front of Aoife, to get her safe behind me. But then I realised she was doing the same thing, to try and get me safe behind her. And we must have got mixed up and I don't know how it happened but suddenly somehow, accidentally, we were holding hands.

And we looked at each other for just a millionth of a second . . .

. . . and then **CRASH!!!** The vent came flying off the wall, and there, inside it, was . . .

Fernando!

"Check it out!" he shouted. "I am crawling through **DUCTS!** I have **LITERALLY ALWAYS WANTED TO DO THIS!**"

"Come on!" shouted Anisha, who was behind him in the duct. "We can get you out this way!"

And Fernando and Anisha hopped down out of the ducts, and even though things were **SUPER SERIOUS**, we all took a second to do a quick Best Friends Secret Handshake. Because come **ON**.

Riyad popped out of the duct too, reading a **BOOK**. Which didn't really seem like a top priority in this situation, but did seem **VERY RIYAD**.

"It's the Operating Manual for the **Teacher-Bots!**" he said. "I ran and got it from Mr Javid's office. It was still in the wrapper, I don't think he's even read it!"

And we all agreed that that seemed about right, because Mr Javid is **VERY LAZY**, when suddenly . . .

KRACCKKK!! The hockey sticks splintered in half

and the doors to the Storage Cupboard **FLEW** open!

"TARGETS IDENTIFIED!" the **Teacher-Bots** chanted. "IT IS US AND THEM! CRUSH! DESTROY! ANNIHILATE!"

"Go! I shouted." "I'll hold them off!"

And with a **FWOOSH** I **FLEW** into the **Teacher-Bots** again, knocking them all back out into the gym and away from my friends . . .

KAPOWW! WHACKKK! KRANGGG! It was just a BLUR of ***ROBOT-PUNCHING***, until suddenly . . .

One of them ***WHACKED*** me with its **CRICKET** bat! I fell down and they all started piling on top of me chanting . . .

"THEY ARE THE ENEMY. IT IS US AND THEM. NOT WITH US, AGAINST US."

And I remembered what Alex had said, about how Us and Them is never a good idea, for anyone. And I thought, it's not bad enough I'm being **ATTACKED** by **EVIL ROBOTS**, I also have to admit Alex was right about stuff?

"NOT WITH US, AGAINST US!" chanted the **Teacher-Bot**.

And it raised its Cricket Bat Arm . . . for the final blow.

All of a sudden a football **FLEW** in from somewhere at SUPER-HIGH SPEED, **WHACKING** the **Teacher-Bot** right in the head and sending it staggering backwards.

"Get 'em!" someone shouted, and I looked round to see . . .

Everyone! Anisha and Fernando and Riyad and Henrik, storming to the rescue! And leading the charge was Aoife! They'd emptied out all the big nets of balls from the Storage Cupboard and were kicking them at the **Teacher-Bots** like a crazy free-for-all Penalty Shootout **OF DOOM!**

"Suck it, teachers!" shouted Fernando, kicking a

basketball **WHAMMMM** into the head of one **Teacher-Bot** and sending it flying.

"Henrik! Over there!" shouted Aoife, pointing at another **Teacher-Bot**. "Four o'clock! *FIRE*!" And Henrik turned and *SLAMMM*, punted a volleyball right at its head.

"It's working!" shouted Anisha, helping me to my feet. "Keep shooting!"

But it wasn't working for long. No matter how many times the **Teacher-Bots** got dinged in the head with volleyballs and basketballs and even **CRICKET** balls, they just kept getting back up again and advancing towards us, yelling **"CRUSH! DESTROY! ANNIHILATE!"**

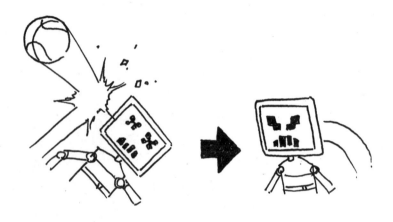

Until . . . Henrik fired a wild shot at one of them but **MISSED**. The ball sailed right past it . . . and into the **GOAL**.

And suddenly all the **Teacher-Bots** STOPPED. And went **"BEEP! ROBOTS 2 – HUMANS 1"**. And went back behind the line, into their half of the pitch.

"What was that?" asked Fernando.

"They're still playing the game!" shouted Riyad from the sidelines, thumbing frantically through the manual. "Even though they're malfunctioning, they're sticking to their core program – they won't stop until the game is over."

"So, wait," said Anisha. "Can we just let them win? And it'd all be over?"

"No!" said Riyad. "Their competitiveness settings are fried! If they win, they'll go completely haywire! They could go on a **RAMPAGE**, start attacking humans everywhere . . ."

"So that means . . .?" said Anisha.

"They have to lose!" said Riyad. "It's the only sure way to complete the program and get them to shut down!"

"So, basically," said Fernando, looking very excited,

"you're saying we have to win this game of football, to **SAVE THE WORLD?**"

"Basically, yes," said Riyad.

"Sweet," said Fernando.

"Okay," said Aoife. "It's first to three. We can do this, we just need two more goals. Freddy, I'm making you an official member of Team Human."

And I wasn't sure about that, because I never asked to be on Team Human, but before I had a chance to protest . . .

One of the **Teacher-Bots** apparently got tired of waiting, because it made a loud electronic whistle sound . . .

. . . and suddenly the game was back on.

CHAPTER 26

The **Teacher-Bots** were all charging towards us again, shouting "BEEP! CRUSH! DESTROY! ANNIHILATE!"

"Leave this to me," I said, in my coolest voice. Because I could suddenly see what I had to do. It was time for me to step up. To be a hero. To save all my friends and prove that robots were good after all and generally make **EVERYTHING OKAY AGAIN**. I walked out in front of the advancing robots, and put a ball down in front of me. This was it. This was **MY MOMENT**.

I ran up to the ball, and kicked it . . .

. . . and it kind of sailed past the **Teacher-Bots**, and bounced off the wall of the gym, and generally went absolutely nowhere near the goal at all.

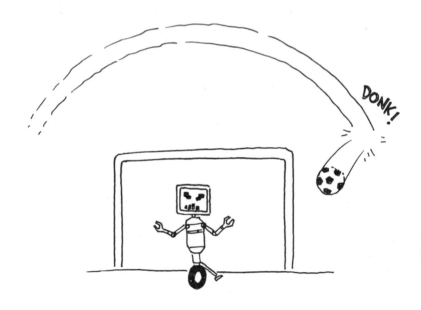

"Nice shot," said Henrik.

"Shut up!" I shouted.

"Anisha!" said Aoife. "Let's do the one-two run — like in that match we had against Stepney Juniors!"

"Got it," said Anisha.

And Anisha and Aoife started running up the pitch, passing the ball between them, keeping it out of reach of the **Teacher-Bots**, in a big zig-zag. Aoife managed to get behind the last of them, and fired it into the goal!

"BEEP!" went the **Teacher-Bots**. "HUMANS 2 – ROBOTS 2!" And they all stopped and went back to their positions again.

"We only need one more!" shouted Aoife. "Come on! We can **DO** this!"

"I can do this!" I shouted, heroically, and frankly a bit annoyed that it was all happening without me. "This is a job," I shouted, running up to take another shot, "for . . ."

And as I ran up I just focused on kicking the ball as **HARD AS I COULD** . . .

And I did! It *FLEW*, like a MISSILE . . .

. . . **STRAIGHT** up in the air, going nowhere near **ANY** of the **Teacher-Bots**, and through the ROOF of the gym with a massive **KROOOM!!!**

"Aaargh!!" I shouted. **"FOOTBALL IS STUPID!"**

"Freddy," said Aoife, "you need to . . ."

"I can do this!" I shouted.

"Freddy!" Anisha shouted back, **CLEARLY ANNOYED**. "You are **BEING AN IDIOT** again.

How many hours of football practice have **YOU** done?"

"Um," I said, ". . . none?"

"Right!" she continued. "And how many hours do you think Aoife's done?"

And I thought of Aoife's room, and the little desk, and the insanely complicated timetable taped to the wall above it.

"Um," I said again, "probably . . . several million?"

"Yeah," said Anisha. "So maybe listen to her. Maybe actually **LEARN** something from **SOMEONE ELSE** for **ONCE!**"

"Jeez," I said. "You don't have to shout."

The robots were getting closer! And this time they were all advancing together, in a big **LINE**, like a **WALL OF ROBOT**, so no one could get past them.

"Okay," Aoife said. "Freddy, listen. Your power is amazing but your control is terrible . . ."

"Hey!" I said.

"Freddy," said Anisha.

"We need to play together, okay?" said Aoife. "**WHEN I SAY**, you need to get past those guys, close to the goal. Can you do that?"

And I was about to protest that I could a lot **MORE** than that. I could do the whole thing myself! But then I saw Anisha's face, and decided to just say "okay."

"Okay!" said Aoife. "Let's go!" And she ran up the left side of the pitch with the ball, shouting at the robots, "Hey! Over here! Primary target over here!"

And all the **Teacher-Bots** started homing in on her, saying "BEEP! PRIMARY TARGET IDENTIFIED!"

And just when they were getting close, she passed the ball across the pitch to Fernando. All the **Teacher-Bots** went "BEEP!" and started chasing him, getting closer and closer . . .

They were nearly on him!
And I heard Aoife shout . . .

FREDDY, NOW !!!

So **FWOOOOSH**, I fired off my **ROCKET BOOSTERS** and **FLEW** over the **Teacher-Bots'** heads, towards their goal. And just when the **Teacher-Bots** were nearly on Fernando, he LOBBED the ball across to me . . .

. . . and I took the shot.

BOOOOM!! Still in mid-air, I kicked the ball with FULL **_MEGA ROBO POWER_** and it went off like a NUCLEAR MISSILE. It **_SMASHED_** straight into the goalie-bot, going **SO HARD** that it lifted him off his wheel . . .

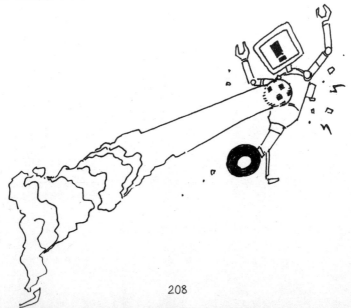

. . . and **THROUGH** the wall of the gym, in a shower
of bricks and dust and concrete . . .

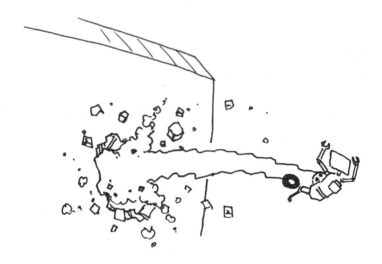

. . . and **ACROSS** the school car park . . .

. . . and finally **DOWN**, with a massive . . .

KRASHH!!!

. . . onto Mr Javid's latest brand new, shiny, super-expensive car.

There was silence for a second. And then Arjun, on the sidelines, clutching his manual, shouted **"GOAL!"** And Arjun blew his whistle.

And all the **Teacher-Bots** paused and looked up, and one said, **"BEEP! GOOD GAME!"**

And then another said **"BEEP! WELL PLAYED, EVERYONE!"**

And then another said, "BEEP! REMEMBER, IT'S NOT THE WINNING OR LOSING THAT COUNTS, IT'S THE TAKING PART!"

. . . and then their screens went blank and they all fell over . . .

For a second, we all just stood there, looking at each other, big grins on our faces, enjoying the weird sudden silence and peace . . .

. . . and then Mr Javid's car EXPLODED.

And we all looked at each other again.

And Fernando yelled,

CHAPTER 28

Well. There was another big assembly the next day and, as you can probably imagine, it was **QUITE EVENTFUL**.

Miss Obasi took the assembly because she had a lot of **NEWS**. She had been organising Industrial Action, where all the teachers were going to go on **STRIKE** to protest about their colleagues being replaced by "untested and unsupervised technological replacements".

". . . which apparently someone didn't even read the **MANUAL** for," she added, giving Mr Javid a **LOOK**.

But they had not needed to be on strike for very **LONG** in the end, because when they arrived at before school to start it, they found . . .

★ **LOTS** of panicking students

★ several **HOLES** in the wall of the gym

★ a smoking **CRATER** in the car park where Mr Javid's car used to be, and

★ all the **Teacher-Bots** powered down and unresponsive, having apparently completely malfunctioned "for reasons unknown", and for which there were **NO CULPRITS** and **DEFINITELY NO WITNESSES**.

214

Aoife and I gave each other a **LOOK**, because we had sworn to each other Never To Speak About ANY **POSSIBLE INVOLVEMENT** that either of us might have **TOTALLY ACCIDENTALLY** had in **ANY EVENTS** that may or may not have happened.

Anyway, the upshot was that all the regular human teachers were back and had their jobs again, and there was Mr Latif, happily eating a sandwich, and the whole school just felt **NICE** and **NORMAL** again.

All the **Teacher-Bots** got taken away, but they didn't scrap them. As Miss Obasi said, the school was lucky enough to have a World-Class Robotics Expert among the parents (**MY MUM**), and she'd promised to take a look and fix them up so they were all safe and useful and worked again, on two conditions:

★   they were used to **SUPPORT** Qualified Human Staff Members, but definitely not to **REPLACE** them, and:

★   someone **ACTUALLY READ THE MANUAL** this time.

And Miss Obasi gave Mr Javid another look. And he was just sitting there looking super grumpy, possibly because now he has to take the bus like everyone else, and whenever kids from school see him on there they all yell **"ALRIGHT SIR! WHERE'S THE CAR?"** and laugh.

At break time I snuck off and quietly used my rocket boosters to fly up into the branches of a big tree down the end of the field. Because I just wanted to be on my own for a bit.

Like, I was glad that everyone was okay, but . . .

. . . . I couldn't help thinking, if people didn't like robots before, having a bunch of them go nuts and actually try to murder people with swords probably wouldn't have helped any. And I was just wondering what school would be like now, and if I could ask my mum to just take me out of it and Home School me or something . . .

. . . when someone said "Hey."

I turned and saw Aoife, climbing up onto the branch.

"Oh! Hey," I said. And then, without even thinking, out came ". . . Sorry."

"What for?" said Aoife.

"Y'know . . ." I said, gesturing in the general direction of the smashed-up gym, and the charred crater in the car park, and everything.

"I hope you're not speaking about the Thing We Agreed Never To Speak About," said Aoife.

"I'm just sorry about . . . all of it," I said. "I shouldn't have said robots were better than humans."

"I shouldn't have said humans were better than robots," said Aoife. "I just . . . I didn't know. I never went to school with a robot before. I didn't know you were . . . you know. Cool."

Cool, I thought.

And we looked at each other, and just then there was a gust of wind and the branch shook, and without thinking about it I reached to grab her to make sure she was okay, and she reached to grab me to make sure I was okay. And before you knew it, somehow, by accident we were holding each other's hands again.

"Hey!" came a voice from down below. "Freddy, are you up there? Are we **PLAYING** or what?"

"Fernando?" I called down, quickly letting go of Aoife's hand. "Wait . . . . what? Playing what?"

"Look, just get down here!" shouted Fernando.

"Race you!" said Aoife, grinning. And she set off down the trunk of the tree like a shot. So I flew back down to the ground with my **ROCKET BOOSTERS**, and saw . . .

Everyone standing around, kicking a football back and forth.

"Football?" I said. "Are you sure that's a good idea?"

"It's just a friendly," said Fernando. "A kick-about. We can play some keepy-uppy or something."

"Um, okay," I said. "So, wait — am I still an honorary member of Team Human? Or do you guys want to come back on Team Robot? Or . . .?"

"Maybe it's time to knock all that 'Team Human, Team Robot' stuff on the head, eh," said Anisha.

"Yeah," said Fernando. "And instead, we can all just be . . . on Team **AWESOME**."

Team Awesome, I thought. With me, and all my friends, and Aoife. That definitely sounded okay.

So we all played keepy-uppy for a bit. And then we invented a new game called **MEGA ROCKET KEEPY-UPPY**, and then after a while we forgot what were were even playing because we were all just laughing too much, and we spent the rest of break messing around and laughing and kicking balls at each other. And no one got hurt or injured at **ALL** . . .

AAAAIIIEEE!!

. . . mostly.

THE END

READ FREDDY'S AWESOME FIRST ADVENTURE IN . . .

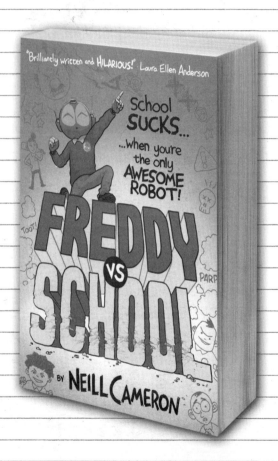

Freddy's awesome robotic **SUPERPOWERS** have been getting him in **TROUBLE!** Mr Javid has told him that if he uses his powers at **SCHOOL** any more, he'll be **EXPELLED!** This is going to be a problem . . .

OUT NOW!

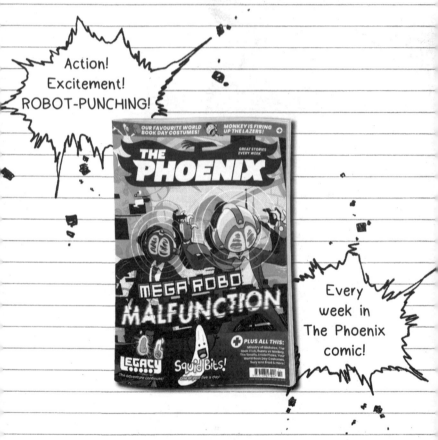

About the Author

Neill Cameron is an award-winning writer and cartoonist. He is the creator of several comic books, including **Mega Robo Bros** and **How To Make Awesome Comics**. Neill's comics appear regularly in **The Phoenix**, the weekly story comic.

Freddy and the New Kid is his second novel starring Freddy, after **Freddy vs School**.